"The child you're carrying is the Sinclair heir." His face was an expressionless mask as he turned back to face her.

"What if it's a girl?" she replied challengingly.

"I already told you I'm the only grandchild—so, girl or boy, as soon as it's born this child will automatically become the Sinclair heir," he bit out tersely. "I'm sure you aren't unaware of what that means."

Luccy had a sinking feeling she really wasn't going to like the rest of this conversation! Not that it had exactly been enjoyable so far, but the way this was going she just knew it was going to get worse....

She frowned. "All it means to me is that my child's father is named Jacob Sinclair the Third."

"Our child will be the Sinclair heir!"

"So you've said. Repeatedly." Luccy grimaced. "But that will only apply until you have other, legitimate children."

"What makes you so sure that I don't intend for this child to be legitimate?" Sin cut in forcefully, those gray eyes once again glittering arctically.

Dear Reader,

It's really wonderful to be part of Harlequin's sixtieth birthday celebrations! As it happens, I've also just celebrated my thirtieth anniversary of writing for Harlequin. It's been a wonderful thirty years: full of love, excitement, fun, adventure—exactly what reading and writing Harlequin Presents® is all about.

I am sure you will join me in wishing Harlequin at least another sixty years of publishing the stories you want to read!

Carole Mortimer

Carole Mortimer

PREGNANT WITH THE BILLIONAIRE'S BABY

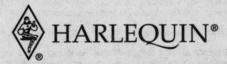

HARLEQUIN®

TORONTO • NEW YORK • LONDON
AMSTERDAM • PARIS • SYDNEY • HAMBURG
STOCKHOLM • ATHENS • TOKYO • MILAN • MADRID
PRAGUE • WARSAW • BUDAPEST • AUCKLAND

Recycling programs
for this product may
not exist in your area.

ISBN-13: 978-0-373-12839-6

PREGNANT WITH THE BILLIONAIRE'S BABY

First North American Publication 2009.

Copyright © 2009 by Carole Mortimer.

www.eHarlequin.com

Printed in U.S.A.

All about the author...
Carole Mortimer

CAROLE MORTIMER is one of Harlequin's most popular and prolific authors. Since her first novel, published in 1979, this British writer has shown no signs of slowing her pace. In fact, she has now published more than 135 novels!

Her strong, traditional romances, with their distinct style, brilliantly developed characters and romantic plot twists, have earned her an enthusiastic audience worldwide.

Carole was born in a village in England that she claims was so small that "if you blinked as you drove through it you could miss seeing it completely!" She adds that her parents still live in the house where she first came into the world, and her two brothers live very close by.

Carole's early ambition to become a nurse came to an abrupt end after only one year of training, due to a weakness in her back suffered in the aftermath of a fall. Instead she went on to work in the computer department of a well-known stationery company.

During her time there, Carole made her first attempt at writing a novel for Harlequin. "The manuscript was far too short and the plotline not up to standard, so I naturally received a rejection slip," she says. "Not taking rejection well, I went off in a sulk for two years before deciding to have another go." Her second manuscript was accepted, beginning a long and fruitful career. She says she has "enjoyed every moment of it!"

Carole lives "in a most beautiful part of Britain" with her husband and children.

"I really do enjoy my writing, and have every intention of continuing to do so for another twenty years!"

CHAPTER ONE

'THIS is really *not* a good idea, Paul!'

Luccy glared up at him as he pinned her against the wall in the hallway outside the hotel restaurant where she had earlier wined and dined him and another senior executive from *Wow* magazine.

Time was when Luccy would have been the one taken out to dinner, but there were too many excellent fashion photographers out there nowadays, all of them hungry for work. With only one prestigious contract with PAN Cosmetics, a subsidiary company of the mega-big Sinclair Industries, to recommend her—a contract that she couldn't be sure would be renewed in three months' time when a photographer like Roy Bailey had decided he also wanted it—Luccy badly needed this assignment with *Wow* if she didn't want to be reduced to taking photographs of babies and weddings.

But she certainly didn't need the assignment with *Wow*—with anyone!—badly enough to go to bed with one of its senior executives to get it.

Admittedly, Paul Bridger, the younger of the two men, had made several suggestive remarks to her during the evening—despite the fact that he had also men-

tioned having a wife and two children at home in
Hampshire. However, Luccy had thought she had
fended off those remarks without too much injury to
pride on either side and both men had excused themselves after the meal with the promise that they would
be in touch.

Except Paul had doubled back and was now proposi-
tioning her after she'd left the restaurant having paid a
huge restaurant bill Harper-O'Neill Ltd could ill afford.

'Oh, come on,' he cajoled now as he pressed closer.
'You know you've been giving me the come-on all
evening.' Paul smiled confidently as he moved his
thighs suggestively against hers.

Luccy inwardly squirmed with distaste. What she
should do was slap Paul's face and tell him exactly
what she thought of him! What she had to do, in order
not to cause a complete scene in a public place, was put
an end to this situation as quietly and quickly as
possible...

She gave what she hoped was a light-hearted little
laugh as she pushed him away playfully. 'I really don't
think your wife would approve, do you?'

Blue eyes narrowed in a face that wasn't unattrac-
tive—just married! 'My wife isn't going to know about
it. Or is she?' he added suspiciously, his hands now
painful on her shoulders as he pinned her even more
firmly against the wall.

Luccy moistened suddenly dry lips. 'That depends—'

'On what?' Paul snarled.

'Excuse me...?'

Luccy's face flamed with embarrassment as she
realised that she and Paul were blocking the hallway

outside the restaurant, and one of the other diners was now waiting to go past them.

Luccy gave him a quick glance, noticing the man's height first, as he was well over six feet. He was probably aged in his mid-thirties, with styled overlong dark hair, and eyes of piercing silver-grey, the suntan—and attractive American drawl—stating that he originated from much warmer climes than England in this wet and overcast June. His black, expensively tailored evening suit and snowy white silk shirt emphasised the broad width of his shoulders, as well as his muscled chest, slim waist, powerful thighs and long, long legs.

The slightly disgusted expression in that piercing grey gaze as it swept over Luccy and Paul wasn't exactly encouraging. But, Luccy decided quickly, she could deal with that later—right now she needed rescuing!

'David! How lovely to see you again!' She gave the man a glowing smile as she took advantage of Paul Bridger's momentary distraction at the interruption to duck under his arm and step away from him, moving to link her arm with the tall American's. 'Paul was just leaving. Weren't you, Paul?' she added pointedly.

'I—' He blinked, scowling darkly as he looked from Luccy to the tall man who stood so arrogantly disdainful at her side. 'Yes, I was just leaving,' he snapped, shooting Luccy one last narrow-eyed glare before striding down the hallway towards the front entrance of the hotel.

Luccy's legs felt strangely weak once Paul had gone, and for a few seconds all she could do was cling to the arm of the man now standing beside her. A man she had never seen before in her life!

A man who now looked down at her with raised brows. '"David"?' he asked dryly.

Luccy gave an apologetic grimace. 'I'm really sorry about all that. A—a work colleague who got out of hand,' she explained—although she seriously doubted, from Paul's last glaring look, that she would ever get any work with *Wow* magazine now! 'Er—do we know each other?' she added. For some reason, the man looked vaguely familiar to her.

As far as Sin was aware he had never met this woman before. He would most certainly have remembered if he had!

Sin had been sitting alone at his table by the window in the hotel restaurant earlier when he'd seen this young woman enter, his attention snared as he'd watched her pause briefly in the doorway to look around the full restaurant before making her way decisively to the table where two men had sat talking together. Sin's mouth had tightened with displeasure as he had acknowledged that his wasn't the only male gaze drawn to the sensual sway of her hips as she walked.

She was probably aged in her late twenties, about five eight in height, Sin would have guessed, with very long silky black hair that gleamed with midnight-blue lights as it swung softly onto her shoulders and curled down the long length of her spine. The deep blue of her eyes was surrounded by long, long lashes of the same ebony colour, her skin a perfect unblemished magnolia, her nose small and straight, and the fullness of her lips glossed the same vibrant red as the knee-length dress she wore. High breasts and that sensuous sway of her hips as she walked seemed to give the impression that was all she was wearing!

Sin's gaze had continued to be drawn to her throughout the evening as she had conversed animatedly with
the two men as they ate their meal. He didn't usually
stare at women he had never met, but there had been
something about this woman, something that had drawn
his gaze back to her time and time again. Not that it had
been his intention of approaching or talking to her, but
then he hadn't been the one to approach or talk to her
now, had he?

He shrugged. 'Maybe you recognise me from the
restaurant?'

Luccy nodded. Now that he mentioned it, she did
remember seeing him sitting alone in the restaurant when
she'd arrived earlier; with his looks it was impossible not
to notice him! But with her future on the line Luccy had
dismissed him from her mind as she had focused all of
her attention on the two executives from *Wow*.

'I really do appreciate your help just now.' She gave
him a bright, dismissive smile.

His hand closed lightly over hers before she could step
away from him. 'You're trembling.' He frowned darkly.

Was she? Yes, she was. But was that because of Paul
Bridger's behaviour just now, or because she was so
aware of the man standing beside her, his hand cool and
yet firm as it covered hers?

Luccy gave a shaky laugh. 'So I am.' She grimaced.
'I just wasn't expecting—that.' She gestured to where
the disgruntled Paul had just left.

The tall American gave her a quizzical look. 'Perhaps
you should sit down for a while? A brandy might help.'

Luccy was starting to feel a little ridiculous; after all,
Paul had only been trying his luck just now. He
wouldn't actually have forced her. Would he…?

'You *are* upset.' The American scowled fiercely as Luccy gave another shiver of reaction. 'I have a bottle of brandy upstairs in my suite—I'm only offering to give you a medicinal brandy,' he added dryly as he obviously saw Luccy's dismayed expression. 'I think you've probably been propositioned enough for one evening, don't you?'

'Sorry!' Luccy exclaimed, knowing she was overreacting. After all, this man needn't have come to her rescue; he could just as easily have exposed her as being a complete stranger to him. 'Luccy,' she invited huskily.

'Excuse me?'

'My name's Luccy.'

'Ah.' He nodded. 'Just Luccy?'

'Just Luccy.' This evening was enough of a mess already, without it becoming publicly known that the photographer Lucinda Harper-O'Neill, contracted to PAN Cosmetics, had been involved in an unpleasant scene in a hotel as prestigious as The Harmony!

Dark brows rose over those pale grey eyes as the American answered her. 'Then I suppose I'm just Sin,' he drawled softly.

Her smile was rueful now. 'Interesting name.'

Sin studied the delicate perfection of Luccy's profile—the deep, unfathomable blue of her eyes, like a flawless sapphire with the light shining behind it, that short nose, the fullness of her mouth, her small pointed chin—before allowing his gaze to move discreetly lower to the creamy swell of her breasts visible above the fitted red gown, her nipples clearly outlined against the flimsy material, as was the slope of her waist and the curve of her hips and thighs.

'Maybe I should just call it a night.' Long dark lashes

lowered onto her creamy cheeks. 'Much as I appreciate your help just now, I'm not sure it would be…sensible on my part to go up to your hotel suite with you.'

To hell with whether or not it was sensible—now that circumstances had allowed him to talk to her, to hear the husky sensuality of her voice, Sin wanted to know this woman better. A whole lot better!

His mouth quirked. 'I'm sure I could get two character references if you're willing to wait here—'

'Now you're making me sound childish!' Luccy protested.

He raised dark brows. 'What do you think? Will you risk it?'

Luccy thought that the way she had completely misread Paul Bridger had shown her just how naïve she was when it came to men. By accepting this man's invitation she could just be jumping out of the frying pan directly into the fire.

She might be well on her way to thirty, but that didn't mean she was in the least sophisticated when it came to reading men. There had only ever been one man in her life in an intimate way, when she was at university seven years ago, and that certainly hadn't been very exciting. So much so that she hadn't been particularly interested in repeating the experience since.

Yet just *looking* at this man—a man called Sin, for goodness' sake!—was exciting!

Oh, for goodness' sake, Luccy, she instantly chided herself again. The Harmony hotel was one of the most exclusive and expensive in London, and this man was a guest here, not a mass murderer. Besides, he was only offering her a glass of brandy to settle her shaken nerves, not a night of unbridled sex—and if by some strange chance he *should* offer the latter, she could always say no; unlike Paul, this man didn't look the type of man who needed to force a woman into his bed!

Nevertheless… 'Just a glass of brandy?'

He smiled. 'Sure.'

Luccy still hesitated, half of her intrigued by this man, the other half—

'There really is no need to be scared, Luccy,' Sin reassured her ruefully.

Luccy bristled resentfully as she realised some of her thoughts must have shown on her face. 'My caution has nothing to do with being scared,' she denied sharply. 'I've just escaped from one awkward situation—'

'You believe I'm trying to get you up to my suite in order to seduce you?' He raised arrogant brows.

'No, of course not!' Luccy's cheeks blazed with embarrassed colour; what a way to treat the man after he had come to her rescue! 'I'm just not in the habit of going to the hotel room of a man I've only just met.' Especially considering the circumstances under which they had met.

The man called Sin shrugged broad shoulders. 'All I'm suggesting is a reviving glass of brandy.'

Was he? Was his invitation really that innocent?

'It's a hotel suite, Luccy,' he added impatiently. 'With its own lounge, and not a bed in sight, I promise.'

Now he was starting to make her feel naïve and unsophisticated. 'Okay, then, I'll come,' she decided, her eyes taking on a glittering determination as she saw the amused slant to that sculptured mouth.

'After you…' Sin indicated for her to precede him to the lifts, his gaze appreciative as the red silk of her gown clung to the thrust of her breasts and the gentle curve of her hips, her red strappy sandals adding to the length of her silkily long legs. Her beauty was all the more stunning because she seemed so completely unaware of just how sexily attractive she was.

But Sin was aware of it. Totally. Especially once they had stepped into the confines of the private lift together, the mirrored walls reflecting back numerous images of Luccy.

'Mmm, nice,' she murmured appreciatively seconds later as they stepped straight out into the luxurious sitting-room of the penthouse suite. 'Are you sure you're just an ordinary hotel guest?' she added teasingly.

'Pretty sure.' Sin nodded. As it happened, he wasn't just a hotel guest at all—he owned the hotel. Or, at least, his family did. As well as owning several more such exclusive hotels around the world, and businesses too numerous to mention.

Not that he *had* any intention of mentioning his family or their businesses to Luccy. In fact, he had been quite happy to fall in with the anonymity of their single name introduction; it was pleasant knowing that this chance meeting with Luccy held no hidden agenda after years of being surrounded by women who might or might not be attracted to him, but who definitely had their covetous eye on his name and wealth.

There had been many women in Sin's life the last eighteen years or so. Beautiful, enticing, intelligent women. But this woman, beautiful, warm, and incredibly sexy, was all the more enticing to *him* because she obviously had no idea of his real identity...

Luccy's eyes were wide as she looked around the opulent luxury of the room. She was sure that the paintings on the walls were originals, and that the gold decoration on the coving above was genuine, as were the tasteful ornaments placed so casually on the antique furniture. The two huge sofas were plushly upholstered, and she thought the blue patterned carpet was probably Persian.

Staying a single night in a suite like this one probably cost as much as she earned in a week—no, a month!

This man—Sin—seemed different in these opulent surroundings too, exuding a powerful sexual magnetism that made Luccy's insides quiver, the quiet strength of his movements as he crossed the room to a tray of drinks giving him the appearance of an elegant predator.

Uh oh!

Maybe this really hadn't been such a good idea after all. For it had never occurred to Luccy that she might not *want* to say no to a night of unbridled sex!

'So what are you doing in London, Sin?' she asked lightly to cover up her nervousness as he swiftly crossed the room carrying the two glasses of brandy.

'Business,' he dismissed as he held out one of the glasses to her, that pale silver-grey gaze fixed steadily on her face as he did so.

'Just business?'

'Mostly, yes.'

Luccy drew in a ragged breath, very much aware that she was probably well out of her league with this man. 'And is your wife in England with you?'

He smiled, his teeth very white and even against the natural tan of his skin. 'That was pretty slick, Luccy.' He gave an appreciative nod. 'But I would hardly have invited you up to my hotel suite if my wife was waiting for me in the bedroom.'

Luccy's sense of unease deepened. 'So is she at home in the States?'

That silver gaze was very direct. 'I'm not married, Luccy.'

'Oh.' She took a reviving sip of the brandy, self-consciously aware that he was watching every movement she made. Luccy felt an answering quiver of awareness down the length of her own spine at being the complete focus of those intense silver-grey eyes.

Which was not supposed to happen, Luccy told herself firmly as she moved away to stand in front of the window and look out at the London skyline.

'Would you like to go outside onto the terrace?' he invited huskily, taking her glass from her hand and placing it on a table with his own before opening the door to outside and then waiting to one side for her to precede him.

Why not? The cool summer air might succeed in cooling Luccy's own sudden heated awareness of him!

Although perhaps not, she realised as Sin, having observed her slight shiver at the sudden breeze, slipped off his dinner jacket and placed it about the bareness of her shoulders. The material was still warm from his own body, and smelled both of an elusively expensive aftershave and something else that was purely, powerfully male. This male.

It also allowed Luccy to appreciate that the wideness of his shoulders owed nothing to tailoring, or the muscled flatness of his chest and stomach to the cut of the white silk shirt, the increase of her pulse rate as she looked at him telling her just how dangerously aware she was of all those things.

'This really is the most incredible view!' she murmured appreciatively as she looked out over the illuminated skyline of London.

'Incredible,' Sin echoed, but he was looking at Luccy and not the view over the terrace.

He stood slightly to the left and behind Luccy as she stood near the four foot high railing, enjoying watching the way the breeze teased the long, dark tendrils of her hair, the moonlight giving a ethereal beauty to the pale oval of her face.

Admittedly, the two of them had met in strange circumstances, and Sin knew nothing about this woman but her name, and yet he knew that he wanted her, that he had from the moment he had looked at her in the restaurant earlier. He wanted to be against her, on her, inside her, with a fierceness he could never remember feeling for any woman before this one.

'Amazingly beautiful,' he said throatily, knowing that he still wasn't talking about the London skyline she looked at so admiringly, that at this moment he could see nothing, was aware of nothing else but the delicately beautiful woman standing in front of him.

Luccy turned slightly, dark brows raised teasingly. 'I didn't even know London hotels had suites like this one!'

'Perhaps they don't.' Sin's teeth gleamed wolfishly in the darkness as he smiled. 'This suite happens to belong to the owner of the hotel,' he explained.

Those incredible blue eyes widened. 'So you know him?'

'Slightly.'

'Well enough to use his suite, at least!'

'At least,' he confirmed non-committally.

Luccy felt even more out of her depth. This man, Sin, was obviously rich as well as arrogantly handsome if he was acquainted with the owners of The Harmony hotel. Which put him well out of range of her normal acquaintances.

'It must be nice to have such influential friends,' she commented lightly.

He shrugged those broad shoulders. 'It has its moments.'

Luccy would just bet that it did!

This really had been the strangest of evenings, she decided ruefully. First she was propositioned by a man she had hoped to work for, and now she had ended up in the hotel suite of a man who was probably rich enough to buy out *Wow* magazine ten times over.

'Perhaps we should go back inside?' she suggested a little breathily as she realised just how close Sin was now standing to her.

Pulse-racingly so.

Maybe she had been working too hard? Maybe she had drunk half a glass of wine too much with her dinner earlier? Maybe seven years was too long to go between physical relationships…?

Whatever the reason, Luccy found she was seriously—tremblingly!—attracted to a man she knew only as Sin. And, what was worse—she could see by the sudden warmth in that silver gaze that Sin was completely aware of that attraction.

'Are you feeling better now?' he murmured.

'A little, thank you.'

Sin became very still as he recognised the temptation of Luccy's pouting lips. After that earlier unpleasantness would she run screaming if he were to kiss her? Nothing too heavy after that lout's behaviour earlier;

Sin just needed to know if the fullness of those perfect lips tasted as good as it looked!

He closed the short distance between them to look down at her in the moonlight. 'May I...?' he asked huskily, holding her gaze for several long seconds before he lowered his head to capture her mouth with his.

Her lips were warm and silky beneath his, with a taste of heated honey. Sin's jacket slid from her shoulders onto the terrace as he deepened the kiss, so he was able to feel each warm curve of her body through the two layers of sheer silk that consisted of her dress and his shirt.

She tasted even better than she looked!

Luccy drew breath back into her starved lungs as Sin's lips finally left hers, having known herself to be lost the moment his arms had moved about her so assuredly.

She trembled in reaction as his lips now trailed across her cheek and down her jaw, to the long column of her throat as he sought and found the area of sensitivity beneath her ear lobe. His tongue moved moistly across her quivering flesh before his teeth nibbled that lobe and created an aching pleasure so exquisite it bordered on pain.

Luccy's breasts felt suddenly full and thrusting, the nipples highly sensitive, and her thighs had suffused with a fierce burning heat that took her totally by surprise. So much so that she knew she had to put a stop to this. Now.

She twisted lightly away from him, her hands resting briefly on his chest as she steadied herself before taking a step back. 'Well, that wasn't supposed to happen,' she muttered uncomfortably.

His gaze was quizzical in the moonlight. 'Are you sorry that it did?'

No, Luccy wasn't sorry. Sorry didn't even begin to describe the emotions this man aroused in her! The truth of the matter was Luccy could never remember feeling such an overwhelming desire to lose herself to the moment. To forget who and what she was and just enjoy the here and now.

It was a realisation that terrified the life out of her!

'Perhaps we should go back inside; I'll finish my brandy and then leave,' she suggested, her heart pounding so loudly in her ears she was sure he must be aware of it too.

Sin looked at her searchingly. His desire for her earlier this evening had been instant, immediate, and, now that he had actually kissed her, held her, his body ached for more. He was pretty damned sure, from her response as he'd kissed her, that Luccy felt the same need too.

'Could we at least go back inside?' she prompted again at his continued silence. 'It's getting a little cold out here, don't you think?' As if to prove her point she shivered a little as she wrapped her arms about the slenderness of her waist.

Sin studied her for several long seconds, aware that Luccy's smile seemed slightly forced, and that her deep blue gaze no longer quite met his.

Not surprising really when she had already fended off the unwanted attentions of one man this evening!

Luccy was right to try and slow things down between them, Sin acknowledged frowningly. And now that they had introduced themselves, there was no reason why he couldn't invite her out to dinner tomorrow.

'Sin?' she pressed lightly.

'Of course we can go back inside, if that's what you want,' Sin acquiesced warmly.

'It is.'

'Are you okay?' Sin asked.

Her smile was definitely strained. 'Fine,' she said.

Sin bent to pick up his jacket before following her inside, knowing that, before she left, he needed to do his utmost to persuade Luccy to see him again…

FORM 004 06/14/95

** RECEIPT **

ORIGIN(E):
KINGSTON ON

DESTINATION:
TORONTO ON

OW SENIOR
$44.73

$42.60 FARE
$2.13 GST
$44.73 CASH

KINGSTON ON
TORONTO ON

TWW

20% REFUND PENALTY

1007-02 KINGSTON 02 072
O/S 440641 05/25/09 11:10 AM
TWW SENIOR CITIZEN
TICKET: 072 346528

COACH CANADA/TRENTWAY
791 WEBBER AVE, PETERBOROUGH, ON, K9J 7B1, (800) 461-7661

GST R898659438

NOT GOOD FOR TRANSPORTATION/NON VALIDE POUR TRANSPORT

TERMS AND CONDITIONS OF CARRIAGE

NOTICE TO SHIPPERS

The Carrier agrees to carry and deliver the packages described hereon upon the terms and conditions prescribed by the proper authority of the province in which this shipment originates and published in the tariff of the Carrier which is open for inspection by the public at the principal office of the Carrier and at the termini of each route over which the shipper agrees by accepting this receipt.

LIABILITY

Liability is limited to ($50.00) for loss or damage howsoever occasioned unless higher value is declared at the time of shipment by the shipper. No claim will be considered unless notice in writing is received within (30) days after the date of acceptance for transportation by the Carrier. If COD, maximum value accepted is $ 1,000.00.

Liability for delay is limited to a refund of express charges.

Claims for consequential loss resulting from loss, damage, misdelivery, failure to deliver, or delay shall not exceed the maximum liability of the Carrier.

CLAIMS

Subject to tariff regulations.

Shipments must meet packaging regulations of the Carrier which also includes the handling and packaging of Dangerous Goods.

PROHIBITED ITEMS include but are not limited to Cash, Negotiable Securities, Bonds or certain DANGEROUS GOODS.

NOTICE TO PASSENGER

BAGGAGE LIABILITY LIMITED TO ($100.00) for loss or damage howsoever occasioned whether through negligence of its agents, employees, or otherwise for each ticket holder unless a greater value has been declared at start of trip. Liability may be increased to a maximum of ($1,000.00) on payment of ($1.00) for each additional ($50.00) of valuation.

Issuing Carrier will be responsible only for transportation on its own lines in accordance with tariff regulations and limitation and assumes no responsibility for any acts or omissions of others occurring within or outside Canada.

NAME_____

SIG._____DATE_____

ADDRESS_____

CHAPTER TWO

'So, Luccy,' Sin murmured softly as he replenished their brandy glasses and set one of them down on the coffee table in front of where she had sat down on one of the sofas, choosing not to sit down himself yet; he couldn't think straight when he was too close to her! 'Why don't we relax and you can tell me a little about yourself?' he invited.

She looked back at him beneath lowered—guarded?— lashes. 'There really isn't anything interesting to tell,' she claimed.

Sin's mouth quirked. 'I somehow doubt that very much,' he contradicted.

She straightened, her breasts thrusting forward as she moved one of her hands and lifted the heavy weight of her hair back over her shoulder, once again drawing Sin's appreciative gaze to the bare expanse of her throat and the swell of those creamy breasts against the red silk.

'You first,' she said.

He shrugged wide shoulders. 'Like you, there isn't anything of interest to tell.'

She gave a rueful smile. 'And, like you, I doubt that very much!'

Sin smiled appreciatively at how neatly she had turned the conversation back onto him. 'Well, I'm obviously American. As were my parents. And their parents before them,' he added dryly.

She nodded. 'Are you an only child, or do you have siblings?'

'Only child. Only grandson, too,' he expanded as he found himself drawn into sitting beside her on the sofa despite his previous decision not to do so.

'Wow.' She grimaced. 'So, no pressure, then?'

Sin smiled in spite of himself. 'As you say, no pressure,' he drawled even as he reached out to pick up a tendril of her long blue-black hair, loving the silky feel of it as he curled it around one of his fingers.

He breathed in the heady scent of her perfume, his senses already aroused by her exotic beauty and the kiss they had shared on the terrace. He knew he should have resisted getting too close to her again so soon after that kiss...

'What brings you to London, Luccy?' he asked in an attempt to clear his mind of passionate thoughts.

'Like you, business,' she said.

Sin nodded. 'And what work do you do?'

She hesitated before answering. Sin was patently not going to tell her much about himself; despite the attraction between them, he obviously wasn't interested in having a close relationship with her. So perhaps it would be better to limit the amount of information she gave him about herself. 'I—why don't you try and guess?' she suggested lightly.

Sin smiled derisively. 'I'm not really into guessing games.'

She regarded him quizzically. 'Oh, come on, it could be fun.'

'Okay.' Sin couldn't resist her mischievous expression. 'A model, perhaps?'

She laughed softly. 'Don't they have to be tall and willowy?'

This woman might not be tall enough to be a model, Sin acknowledged, but she was certainly stunningly beautiful enough to be one.

He relaxed back against the sofa. 'So not a model, then?'

'No.' She smiled.

Sin shook his head. 'I somehow can't see you in an office.'

Luccy frowned. 'Why not?'

He raised a mocking eyebrow. 'If I had a secretary that looked like you I would never get any work done!'

'Isn't it a little chauvinistic of you to assume a woman has to be a secretary if she works in an office?' she teased.

Sin gave a self-deprecating grimace. 'Hmm, you have a point.'

Luccy's earlier tension started to leave her as she realised she was quite enjoying this teasing conversation.

He shrugged. 'Okay, so you work in an office…'

'Actually, no, I don't.'

He frowned. 'Is it always this difficult to get a straight answer from you?'

Not usually, no, Luccy acknowledged ruefully. But she was loath to confide too much about herself. As well as her earlier concerns on a personal level, she doubted the management of PAN Cosmetics would appreciate it if the incident between herself and Paul Bridger ever became public knowledge. Jacob Sinclair, the owner of

Sinclair Industries, was very strict concerning his policy of no bad publicity. So much so that it was actually written into employees' contracts, including the one Luccy had signed with PAN Cosmetics the previous year.

Usually Luccy was completely professional when it came to her work—it really wasn't her fault that men like Paul Bridger couldn't behave in the same way!

And the situation she now found herself in? What woman in her right mind would manage to extricate herself from one potentially dangerous situation only to land herself in another one that could prove equally disastrous? In fact, more so, because Luccy hadn't been attracted to Paul Bridger, whereas she was definitely attracted to Sin.

As that kiss outside on the terrace had proved…

'Why are you so interested?' She frowned at Sin's persistence.

'Because everything about you interests me,' he drawled huskily.

Luccy felt the heat enter her cheeks as she easily read the expression in his eyes. This man didn't just want to know about her—he wanted *her*!

She swallowed hard. 'I'm a receptionist. To a photographer.' Not completely untrue; she did act as her own receptionist on occasion, usually when Cathy was at lunch or off sick.

His brows rose. 'Anyone I would have heard of?'

Only if she was very unlucky!

'I doubt it,' she dismissed.

'And that guy earlier—'

'Paul?'

Sin nodded. 'You said he's a work colleague?'

She had said that, hadn't she? How complicated things became when you told just one little exaggeration of the truth!

She shrugged. 'He's more of a prospective client, actually. My boss is out of town so it was left to me to do the wining and dining this evening,' she added lamely.

Sin nodded. 'And do you have a husband, and possibly children, too, waiting for you at home?' He was beginning to think that Luccy's one-name introduction, and her aversion to talking about herself, showed all the classic signs of a married woman out for a night on the town.

Her mouth, that deliciously tempting mouth, curved into a rueful smile. 'No husband, and certainly no children,' she assured him.

'And Luccy is short for…?' Sin was willing to give her the benefit of the doubt concerning a husband and children, a glance at her left hand confirming that there was at least no indentation to the third finger, or evidence of slightly paler skin where a ring might have been hastily removed. He drew the line at becoming involved with a married woman.

'It isn't short for anything,' she said mendaciously as she shook her head. 'And as we obviously aren't going to meet again after tonight, I really don't see the relevance of any of these questions, do you? Or their answers.'

This man really didn't need to know that her full name was Lucinda Harper-O'Neill. Or that she was a photographer, primarily in advertising, with her own studio and apartment right here in London.

'We can't know that yet.'

Luccy gave him a startled glance. 'Can't know what?'

'Whether or not we're going to see each other again. There's no reason why we shouldn't. I come to London quite regularly—'

'And I'm not about to become your "regular London girl"!' Luccy informed him slightly incredulously. 'Look.' She placed her brandy glass down on the coffee table in front of them, releasing her hair from his caressing fingers as she did so. 'I really am grateful to you for—for rescuing me from a very awkward situation earlier, but I'm not grateful enough to hop into bed with you!'

His gaze was lightly teasing. 'But we aren't in a bed.'

'We aren't going to be in one, either,' Luccy told him firmly.

'Maybe not tonight—'

'Not ever,' Luccy insisted flatly.

'How can you be so sure of that?'

She couldn't—that was the problem! Each minute—second!—that passed, she only became more aware of this man. 'Sin—'

'Luccy,' he came back softly even as he moved along the sofa so that their thighs touched, his arm along the back of the sofa behind her as he easily held her gaze with the intensity of his.

To say Luccy was unnerved by his close proximity was an understatement. She was completely overwhelmed by his sheer physical magnetism—and the heat of the desire that suddenly burned in those silver-grey eyes as he looked at her.

Her breath caught in her throat as he lifted a hand to cup and hold her chin, his gaze still fixed intently on hers as he gave her one last chance to tell him no.

Which Luccy already knew she wasn't going to be able to do!

In fact, she had a feeling that every moment since she had first looked up and seen him standing in the hotel hallway had all been leading to this very point.

'I'm aware of how upset you were earlier, so we won't let this go any further than you want it to, okay?' he assured her gruffly as Luccy stared up at him in fascination.

She moistened dry lips. 'Okay,' she breathed tremulously, having absolutely no will to resist anyway as Sin lowered his head towards her and his lips claimed hers in a kiss of such gentleness that it made Luccy ache inside. She had known from that single kiss out on the terrace that it was going to be like this if Sin ever touched her again.

Luccy groaned low in her throat even as her body curved into his, finding herself unable to do anything else but respond as she felt the heat of Sin's body through his shirt as she reached up to grasp his shoulders, her own body flaring and coming tinglingly alive as the tips of her breasts responded to that heat. Sin seemed to take her response as acquiescence as his mouth suddenly hardened demandingly on hers.

Every other thought fled her mind as Sin's mouth continued to plunder hers, tongue questing, stroking, before thrusting deep, drawing Luccy into a swirling maelstrom of emotions and needs, her nipples actually aching now, burning, wanting—

Luccy dragged her lips from his to groan low in her throat as she felt Sin's hand against her naked breast, having no idea when he had slid the zip of her gown down her spine, and not caring either as he cupped and held her before finding that thrusting tip with light, caressing fingertips.

'You can stop me at any time,' he promised huskily.

Luccy couldn't answer him. She knew she should probably take him up on his offer to stop now, but her body was firmly intent on having its own way. She couldn't think when his caresses drove her wild with wanting more, needing more, Sin obligingly giving her more as his skilful hand became more demanding and his head moved lower to draw the tip of her other breast into the heated cavern of his mouth.

Luccy sank back against the cushions of the sofa, her body on fire, a deep aching need between her quivering thighs as Sin continued to make her burn with desire.

Sin had meant it when he told her he would stop at any time, but he was fast losing control, no longer sure he would be able to stop!

His gaze was hot and hungry as he raised his head to look at Luccy. At the twin peaks of her breasts with those rose-tinted tips and the flushed beauty of her face as he ran the pad of his thumb across one of those pouting nipples before once more slowly lowering his head to claim it with his lips and mouth. Immediately he felt her hips move restlessly beneath him with a greater, wilder need.

His hand moved from her breast to her knee, her skin as soft as velvet. He gently stroked along the length of her thigh before sliding under the soft silk of her gown to touch the delicacy of her hip bone, the flatness of her stomach, his touch telling him that he had been wrong about her being completely naked under the red silk gown; she was wearing the briefest scrap of lace, her curls already damp with her need as he cupped her there before seeking the heated warmth beneath that lace.

Luccy cried out at the first touch of Sin's hand

against the ultra-sensitive core of her arousal, her body seeming to melt as he stroked her there, his fingers moving in a rhythmic caress. His mouth moved from her breast to once more claim her lips, his tongue mimicking the rhythm of his fingers.

It felt as if Sin were everywhere all at once. Above her. Beside her. Inside her.

Luccy wanted him deeper inside her, hungered for his possession as his fingers caressed but didn't quite enter her. Luccy writhed, lifting her hips to enable him to remove that scrap of lace, silently pleading with him to satisfy her torturous need. She cried out with pleasure as he finally gave her what she wanted. Luccy's eyes widened as she felt the intensity of her pleasure increase to unbearable heights. Dear God, she was going to—

Luccy groaned low in her throat, eyes closing, desperately pulling his shirt open before she dug her fingers deep into Sin's naked muscled shoulders as the pleasure consumed her, filled her, his ravenous mouth on hers even as she convulsed about those thrusting fingers. Nothing else mattered at that moment except that she didn't ever want him to stop, wanted, ached, for this pleasure to go on and on.

Sin wrenched his mouth from hers to move lower, to give Luccy more as he once again drew one of her pink nipples into his mouth. He felt her back arch as she once more lost herself totally to that pleasure.

He lifted his head to look at her, her breasts full, the nipples pouting a dusky pink now from the ministrations of his mouth and tongue. She groaned as Sin gently parted her legs, before lowering his head and suckling the hardened nub nestled there as her groans turned into a pleading mewl.

Sin dealt quickly and efficiently with the fastening of his trousers as he knew that he couldn't wait a moment longer to sheath himself inside her.

Luccy groaned in protest as his mouth left her, that groan turning to a soft aching sound as she felt the tip of his hardened shaft rubbing against her before slowly, inch by pleasurable inch, he entered her.

He was big and hard, steel encased in velvet, his hands moving to cup her bottom as he began to slowly move in and out of her. Luccy's eyes closed in ecstasy at each thrust, her hand moving down to draw him deeper inside her as those thrusts became fiercer, his mouth once more claiming hers as she felt him tighten, harden, swell inside her before climaxing long and deliciously inside her, inciting wave after wave of new, totally uncontrollable pleasure.

Luccy returned slowly to a sense of who she was, where she was, and who she was with, never having experienced anything so wild and wonderful in her life before, her body still quivering from each pleasurably memorable caress.

She was Lucinda Harper-O'Neill, photographer for PAN Cosmetics, and she was lying half naked on a sofa in a hotel suite, her body still intimately—very intimately!—entwined with a man called Sin...

How had this happened?

She had spent the last seven years without even thinking about becoming physically involved with anyone, too engrossed in making a name for herself as a photographer to have room for anything else in her life. So what was it about Sin that had changed all that? Why him? What—?

'I've always found self-recriminations after the event

to be less than constructive,' Sin advised quietly as he felt the sudden tension in the woman beneath him. He gave her a few seconds to let his words sink in before raising his head to look at her.

If anything she looked even more beautiful with that slightly bewildered look in those amazing blue eyes, her lips swollen from the fierce intensity of their kisses, and there was a rosy flush to her cheeks.

Sin felt no less bewildered himself by the wildness of their lovemaking, could never remember being so aroused by a woman—any woman—that he had almost ripped his own clothes off in his need to join his flesh with hers.

In fact, he still had most of his clothes on. Both of them did.

His smile was rueful as he raised one of his hands to lightly caress her flushed cheek. 'Let's finish undressing, hmm, take a shower, and leave all conversation until later,' he suggested gently.

Luccy didn't want to have a conversation at all with this man! She didn't want to have anything with him, and was utterly mortified by what she had just allowed to happen.

She wasn't the type of woman to indulge in a one-night stand with a man who completely swept her off her feet. Or, at least, she hadn't been...

Regroup, Luccy, she instructed herself firmly. Gather your scattered wits together and just try to come out of this situation with some of your dignity intact.

She kept her gaze on Sin's muscular chest—dear God, she had almost ripped his shirt off him minutes ago!—as she moistened her lips before speaking, the gesture not in the least reassuring as she instantly felt the sensitivity of their bruised fullness. 'I don't believe a post-mortem after the event is necessary, either,' she told him evenly.

'No post-mortem, Luccy,' he assured her, gently stroking the hair at her temple now. 'But maybe we could reassess your earlier decision not to become my "regular London girl"?' he teased.

Her eyes widened as she looked up at him. Sin wanted to see her again? This wasn't just some one-night thing to him while he was in London?

She swallowed hard. 'I—could I take a shower first—alone—and think about that?'

He frowned darkly. 'You don't want us to meet again?'

All Luccy wanted right now was to be alone for a few minutes. She couldn't think around this man!

'I need to shower first,' she insisted huskily.

'But not together?' He voiced his disappointment.

She would hardly be able to think while naked in the shower with an equally naked—totally distracting—Sin!

'Luccy?' Sin prompted as he sensed her hesitation.

She avoided his gaze. 'If you don't mind, I've always preferred to shower alone.'

Sin did mind; he could imagine nothing he would enjoy more at this moment than soaping her body all over before making love to her again under the hot spray of the shower. Neither was he particularly happy that she wanted to think about seeing him again.

What they had just shared had been extraordinary. Amazing.

But he appreciated it might have happened a little too suddenly for Luccy—for him too, if he was honest! But this was certainly not a casual one-night stand for him; Sin had every intention of seeing Luccy again whenever he was in London. Often.

But the comfort of a silk-sheeted bed in half an hour or so, when they were both showered and refreshed, would probably be more reassuring for Luccy. After all, they had the rest of the night to enjoy each other. All day tomorrow too, if Sin rescheduled his meetings. Maybe he would just cancel them indefinitely; Luccy was what interested him at the moment. Luccy, and getting to know each and every thing about her.

'Fine,' he agreed. 'I'll open a bottle of champagne and take it through to the bedroom while you're in the bathroom, and then take a quick shower myself before joining you.'

Not too quick, Luccy hoped—because she already knew that no amount of time in the shower was going to change the fact that while Sin was taking his own shower she had every intention of leaving this suite, and the hotel.

And never seeing Sin again…

CHAPTER THREE

'I WON'T be a moment,' a disembodied voice called from the adjoining room as Sin stepped into the reception area.

The photographic studio, Sin would guess, eyes narrowed as he stood patiently waiting in the outer office. It was ultra-modern, all chrome, white and black furniture, with framed photographs five feet square on the pristine white walls, also in black and white, but excellent none the less.

As he would have expected.

He already knew that Lucinda Harper-O'Neill was a woman who excelled at everything she did, including her career as a photographer.

'I'm really sorry to keep you waiting,' that disembodied voice—Lucinda's voice?—called out again. 'My receptionist has just gone to lunch…' That voice trailed off in a strangled gasp as Lucinda Harper-O'Neill came to an abrupt halt in the doorway, her face paling even as Sin turned to look at her with coolly enquiring silver-grey eyes.

At the woman who, three nights ago, had introduced herself to him only as Luccy.

She wasn't wearing red today, her loose silk blouse the same deep sky-blue as her eyes, and pale blue jeans hugging the slimness of her hips and long, long legs. Her blue-black hair wasn't sexily loose today, either, but secured on her crown, leaving only a wispy fringe on her creamy forehead above those wide, disbelieving eyes, the minimum of make-up on the pale oval of her face, with no enticing deep red gloss on those pouting lips.

Luccy stared aghast at the man who stood so chillingly silent across the room as he continued to look at her with those cold, unrelenting silver-grey eyes. His silence seemed to contain an air of menace, and the expertly tailored dark grey suit he wore, with a white shirt and neatly knotted silver tie, did nothing to dispel the underlying air of a tiger stalking its prey.

Sin!

What was he doing here?

More to the point, how had he known to come to the photographic studio of Lucinda Harper-O'Neill in order to find the woman he knew only as Luccy?

Why had he even *wanted* to find her? Hadn't the fact that she had so abruptly left his hotel suite three nights ago been enough of a hint that she had no interest in seeing him again?

The silence between them, icily arctic on Sin's part, tense on Luccy's, was becoming unbearable! But not so unbearable that she intended being the first one to break it…

Something that Sin seemed aware of as his mouth thinned. 'Lucinda Harper-O'Neill, I presume?' he drawled with agonising mockery.

Luccy's eyes narrowed. Obviously she was Lucinda

Harper-O'Neill. The real question was, how did he know that?

She made a dismissive movement of her shoulders as she stepped fully into the reception area to sit down behind the empty desk, determined not to be cowed by this man's unexpected appearance at her place of work. 'What can I do for you, Sin?'

He gave a smile completely lacking in humour. 'The way I remember it, Luccy, you've already done quite a lot for me already.'

Colour warmed her cheeks, a mixture of anger and embarrassment, her eyes glittering with the former emotion as she glared up at him.

How typical of a man to refer so blatantly to what happened between them in his hotel suite three nights ago! Although it hadn't been a memory that Luccy had found too easy to forget, either...

Although she had tried. She really had. She'd inwardly cringed with self-recrimination every time she so much as thought about the physical intimacy she had shared with him. Damn it, Sin probably knew Luccy's body more intimately than she did!

'Very funny,' she snapped scathingly. 'I thought you would have returned to the States by now?'

He shrugged those broad shoulders. 'Something else came up.'

Something to do with finding her, perhaps? 'Well, as nice as it is to see you again, Sin,' she lied, 'I really am very busy today. So if there is nothing else you need to say to me I really do have to get on with some work.' She looked up at him challengingly.

She was certainly a cool one, Sin acknowledged with grudging admiration.

But, unfortunately for Luccy, he had no intention of leaving here today without getting answers to several pertinent questions. He'd thought of little else but finding her again, talking with her, for the last three days.

Sin had known a lot of women in his thirty-five years, had gone to bed with quite a lot of them too, and never once before had he completely lost control in the way that he had with this woman.

Or felt as angry with any of them as he had with Luccy when he'd come back from the shower that night and found her gone.

Enquiries the following morning had revealed that the table in the restaurant the evening before had been booked to Harper-O'Neill Ltd, the representative of that company joined by two guests from *Wow* magazine.

It hadn't taken too long after that to ascertain that the photographer Lucinda Harper-O'Neill had represented herself; the names 'Luccy' and 'Lucinda' had been too much of a coincidence for it not to be the same person, proving that Luccy had lied to Sin when she'd told him she worked for a photographer—she *was* the photographer.

Unfortunately for Luccy, Sin's enquiries hadn't stopped there—he had also had a very interesting conversation with Paul Bridger, one of the senior executives with *Wow* magazine, earlier this morning. A conversation that had resulted in Sin questioning exactly when Luccy had realised he'd seemed familiar to her that following evening. Before or after he'd come across her with Bridger? After his conversation with Bridger, Sin was betting on it being before. Long before…

There had certainly been no way Sin intended returning to New York until he had seen Lucinda Harper-O'Neill again!

His movements were unhurried now as he strolled over to the chair facing the desk to lower his long length into it before looking across at her with cool deliberation. 'Go ahead and finish up your work. I'm in no hurry,' he assured her quietly.

Luccy frowned her frustration with his relaxed attitude—she was even more tense now than when she had first walked out of her studio and seen him just standing there. 'I told you, I'm busy—'

'Then I'll wait until you're finished,' he persisted evenly.

There was no way that she could go back into her studio and continue working when she knew Sin was sitting out here waiting for her like that stalking, lethally dangerous tiger he so reminded her of!

'What is it you want from me, Sin?' she demanded impatiently.

'Didn't the fact that I left that night tell you that I have no interest in pursuing a relationship with you?'

It hadn't even occurred to her that Sin would attempt to track her down in this way. And for what purpose? Surely he had to realise that she considered what had happened between them to have been a mistake on her part? A mistake she had no intention of repeating!

He relaxed back in the chair as he continued to look across at her with narrowed, unfathomable grey eyes. 'It told me that you had—finished with me. For the moment...'

Luccy didn't like the insult she could hear in his tone. 'I have no idea what you're talking about,' she said as she stood up to glare down at him, too restless to remain seated any longer. 'Now I really think it's past time that you left, Mr—'

'Formality between us seems—a little out of place, in the circumstances, don't you think?' he put in mockingly.

Luccy huffed her frustration. 'I would prefer it. And what I would really prefer is for you to just leave.'

'Not possible, I'm afraid,' Sin returned calmly, icily. 'Not until you've given me a satisfactory explanation for your behaviour three nights ago.'

'*My* behaviour?' Luccy gave him a bewildered look. 'Weren't you there too?'

'Oh, yes, I was there,' he acknowledged. 'Suitably intrigued. But that was the point, wasn't it?'

'The point of what?' Luccy was fast approaching a feeling of unreality.

They had met, made love together, an action they obviously both regretted; what else was there left for them to talk about?

'I could always telephone the police and have you forcibly removed,' she threatened.

'You could try, I suppose,' Sin agreed with an unconcerned shrug of his shoulders. 'Although that might be a little embarrassing for you when I explain to them that this is merely a lovers' tiff.'

'We are *not* lovers,' she told him forcibly.

His mouth twisted. 'Oh, but we are, Lucinda—'

'My name is Luccy!' she cut in vehemently. 'And, no, we most certainly are not!'

She really did have the most beautiful eyes, Sin acknowledged distractedly, of the deepest, loveliest sky-blue, and fringed with the longest, thickest black lashes he had ever seen.

In fact, as he knew intimately, this woman was beautiful all over...

Too much so for him to have simply walked away without finding out more about her. Although a part of him now wished he had just left that night as a pleasant memory. Instead of what it really was!

His mouth tightened. 'If you really believe that, Luccy, then your memory is much more conveniently accommodating than mine.'

No, it wasn't—because Luccy could remember every single intimate detail of their time together in this man's hotel suite.

Every. Single. Intimate. Detail.

Her breasts tingled uncomfortably just being in the same room with him again, and the heated awareness between her thighs was distracting too.

'Oh, please,' she scorned. 'Let's not get carried away and act as if that night really meant anything to you!'

'You think not?'

Luccy gave an impatient shake of her head. 'Probably the only thing that bothers you about that night is that I walked away from you at the end of it!'

He became very still, eyes narrowed to steely slits as he studied her, once again looking like that tiger with the sheathed but ready-to-pounce claws. 'Why did you do it, Luccy?' he finally asked softly.

'It was an impulse. A reckless impulse!' She sighed. 'It certainly isn't something I'm particularly proud of—'

'That's something, I suppose,' Sin acknowledged hardly.

Luccy raised bewildered brows. 'Exactly what are you implying?'

'Why don't you tell me?' he invited, no longer relaxed in his chair as he sat forward.

'Probably because I have no idea what you're talking about!'

Sin had never been as intrigued by any woman as he had been that night with Luccy—or Lucinda Harper-O'Neill, as she had turned out to be. Except *he* hadn't been the one indulging in intrigue!

Although he somehow doubted that night had worked out quite the way Luccy had thought it would; Sin was experienced enough to know that her physical response when they'd made love had been too wild, too out of control, to be in the least bit faked.

Luccy's expression became guarded. 'I've already told you that night was a mistake, that we should both just forget about it.'

'Is that really what you intend doing, Luccy—forgetting about it?' Sin asked.

She gave a puzzled frown. 'I've already said it is.'

Sin inclined his head. 'So you have. The only problem is that I don't believe you.'

'You don't—!' Why hadn't she seen how overbearingly arrogant this man really was? Luccy berated herself fiercely.

Overbearing, yes…

Arrogant, too.

But still pulse-racingly attractive in spite of all that!

Luccy abruptly pulled herself together. 'I don't have the time to sit here and talk nonsense with you. I have work I need to do in my studio. But I'm sure that if you insist on staying, my receptionist will be only too happy to get you a cup of coffee or something when she gets back from lunch—' She broke off, her eyes widening at the speed with which Sin had moved so that he now stood beside her, his fingers clamped like steel about the slenderness of her wrist preventing her from moving away. 'Let go of me, Sin,' she ordered vehemently.

She didn't like him touching her. Didn't like the way she felt when he touched her.

'Just get it over with, Luccy,' he grated harshly. 'Tell me exactly why you went to bed with me.'

She shook her head. 'As you pointed out so succinctly at the time, we didn't actually go to bed!'

He didn't answer her, merely continued to hold her gaze as his thumb moved caressingly across her wrist at the exact point where her pulse was beating. Erratically.

Luccy turned her gaze away from his, very aware of the warm lethargy that was creeping over her body. Of the increased tingling of her breasts as her nipples pressed against the silky material of her blouse. Of the raw ache she felt pressing inside her, urging her to curve her body against the heat of this man's powerful chest and thighs.

This man was *sin* incarnate…!

Luccy had convinced herself over the last few days that she had to have imagined the physical fascination this man held for her, that her behaviour in his hotel suite had been a momentary aberration, that if she ever saw him again she would once again see him only as the man who had helped her out of a difficult situation, rather than the man she had also made love with.

Unfortunately, now that she was seeing him again Luccy couldn't deny her completely physical response to him or the memory of the intimacies the two of them had shared. The way this man had kissed and touched her. Been inside her. Given her such overwhelming pleasure with each measured stroke of his body...

Sin was caught completely unaware as Luccy wrenched her wrist from his grasp to move abruptly away from him, frowning slightly as he realised that there would be bruises later on the pale delicacy of her skin. Bruises she obviously preferred rather than suffering his touch a moment longer.

'I don't remember asking *you* for an explanation about your own behaviour that night!' she exclaimed.

'Maybe because you already know it was because you deliberately set out to make me want you!' Sin rasped.

'Past tense?' she taunted.

'For you or for me?' Sin was stung into retorting, very aware of the way she had been unable to stop herself responding to him seconds ago.

And the way his own body had responded to her proximity. Was still responding to it...

'Oh, definitely past tense as far as I'm concerned, yes!' Luccy declared.

Sin knew she was lying. To herself as well as to him. He knew when a woman's response to him was genuine, when her climax was out of her control—and, no matter what she might choose to tell herself now, he knew that Lucinda Harper-O'Neill had been totally out of control three nights ago.

'Would you like me to prove otherwise?' he challenged mildly.

Her eyes widened in alarm before she quickly masked the emotion with a challenging rise of her chin. 'You could try, I suppose,' she accepted. 'If, that is, you enjoy the experience of making love to a woman who doesn't want you?'

'Oh, you want me, Luccy,' he said with certainty. But he knew they were getting nowhere with this conversation, were just going round and round in circles without actually getting to the truth. And Sin was determined, one way or another, to know the truth about that night.

'We need a little more privacy than this studio provides in order to discuss this further,' he told Luccy evenly. 'I'm going back to my hotel now, but I will expect you to arrive there some time later this evening.'

Her eyes widened, her tone incredulous. 'You can *expect* all you like—'

'If you don't come to the hotel, Luccy, then I will have no choice but to come back here again tomorrow— and if I'm forced into doing that, then I will simply continue to remain here until you give me the explanation I want,' he warned her grimly.

'I have no idea what explanation you want from me!'

'Oh, I think you do.'

She frowned. 'You don't scare me, Sin—'

'No?'

No, this man didn't scare her, Luccy acknowledged with a frown; but the determination in his voice was certainly daunting, and was more of a promise than a threat...

She drew in a ragged breath. 'No,' she confirmed firmly.

He shrugged those wide, powerful shoulders before strolling with a total lack of concern to the door. 'I'll expect you about seven-thirty.' It was a statement rather than a question.

Her mouth set stubbornly. 'I have a date this evening.'

'Break it!' he rasped harshly, silver eyes suddenly glittering dangerously.

Luccy gasped. At The Harmony hotel this man had been charming and incredibly sexy. He was still the latter, unfortunately, but the charm was definitely gone, leaving in its stead a man of compelling, indomitable will.

Why hadn't she seen this cold, implacable man behind that charm three days ago?

She shook her head. 'I don't think I want to do that.'

His smile was chilly and humourless. 'Oh, I really think you'll find that you do,' he taunted.

Luccy's eyes widened at his continued arrogance. 'You're mistaken—'

'Luccy, I believe you only have—what?—a couple of months left to run on your photography contract with PAN Cosmetics, a contract you very badly need to be renewed before you start to flounder financially, if not professionally,' Sin cut in, knowing by the way her eyes widened that he had surprised her with his knowledge of her financial status. He intended surprising her with a lot more than that before the day was over!

'How do you—? You had no right to delve into my financial affairs!' Luccy exclaimed with horror as she realised that was exactly what he had done.

'What happened between us the other evening gave me that right,' Sin announced.

'No!'

'Oh, yes, Luccy,' he ground out. 'I'm sure you would much prefer it if your contract with PAN were to be renewed, wouldn't you?'

Luccy blinked dazedly. How did this man know so much about her? And what business was it of his, anyway?

She glared at him. 'And what if I would?'

Sin couldn't help but admire the way this woman

continued to defy him. Pointlessly so. But he admired her defiance anyway.

He topped her by at least seven inches, the delicacy of her bone structure showing that he probably weighed almost twice as much as she did too. Yet she was so totally, angrily defiant; she reminded him of a small cat hissing a warning at a lion to stay off her territory.

His mouth tightened. 'Isn't it obvious?'

'Not to me, no.'

'It's time to stop playing games, Luccy,' Sin warned icily.

'I'm not playing games!'

'I agree, blackmail can never be considered anything as light-hearted as a game—'

'*Blackmail!*' Luccy took a shocked step back at the accusation.

He arched mocking brows. 'Perhaps you would prefer it if I used the term "leverage"?'

'Now you just listen to me—'

'You have it all wrong, Luccy—*you* will be the one listening to me,' Sin cautioned in a coldly chilling voice. 'Whatever you think the other night was about, whatever *leverage* you think you may have gained by making love with me, I advise you to just forget it. I can assure you, I have no intention—'

'Get out!' Luccy ordered shakily. 'Just get *out!*'

His mouth thinned. 'Will you be coming to my hotel later?'

She glared at him. 'Certainly not!'

Sin gave a shrug. 'Then I guess I'm not leaving, after all.'

Her eyes sparkled like twin sapphires. 'Are you threatening me?' she finally breathed softly.

'No more than you intended blackmailing me,' Sin assured her smoothly.

She shook her head. 'I have no absolutely *no* idea what you're talking about.'

'Try a little harder, Luccy.'

Her frown was pained. 'You're deluding yourself if you think I have any intention of so much as seeing you again.'

Beautiful didn't even begin to describe this woman, Sin allowed ruefully. She was stunningly lovely. Very intelligent. Extremely—arousingly—sexy. Even now...

'I believe at the moment you're the one who is deceiving yourself,' he said huskily.

She blinked. 'I beg your pardon?'

Sin felt an overwhelming compulsion to shake this woman, to leave her as confused as she had left him when he'd come out of the bathroom to find her gone.

'I—what are you doing?' she gasped as Sin crossed the room in two long strides, her eyes wide and wary as she looked up at him as he now stood only inches away from her.

A humourless smile curved his lips. 'You're trembling again, Luccy,' he murmured. 'Why is that?' He quirked dark brows over taunting grey eyes. 'Is it because you are frightened of me, after all?' he taunted. 'Or are you trembling because you think I might touch you again, and you're perhaps a little—just a little—apprehensive of your own response?'

Those blue eyes flashed with temper. 'You egotistical, arrogant son-of-a—'

'I don't believe insulting my mother is going to help this situation,' he cut in.

'I hate y—' Her words were cut off as Sin reached

out to cup either side of her face before his mouth firmly claimed hers.

His mouth was hard, demanding, punishing against hers. Sin barely registered the pummelling of her tiny fists against his chest as she fought to release herself.

She continued to fight for several long seconds before the pummelling slowly stopped and her lips softened beneath his, her body seeming to become liquid flame as it melted into his.

Dangerously so.

Luccy's breasts were pressed against the muscled hardness of Sin's chest, the soft curve of her stomach against his arousal, an arousal that pulsed, burned, with a rapidly spiralling need.

And then his lips softened against hers, sipping, tasting now, inciting an even deeper hunger inside her.

What was it about this man that made her respond in this way?

Luccy had absolutely no idea, but much more of this and she knew that when Cathy returned from her lunch break in a few minutes she was going to be met with the shock of seeing her employer making love to a strange man on top of her desk!

Luccy's face was flushed, her lips slightly bruised-looking, her eyes glittering furiously when Sin finally raised his head to look down at her in slow appraisal.

'No, I don't believe you hate me, Luccy,' he said. 'And hopefully, given time, you'll come to realise that, although I like a certain amount of—spirit, in my women, I actually prefer the way you were the other night rather than having to fight you into submission.'

She gasped. 'You *arrogant*—'

'I believe we've already more than adequately

covered that aspect of my nature,' he dismissed in a bored voice. 'Seven-thirty this evening,' he bit out firmly, taking his leave this time before Luccy could argue any further.

As he was sure that she had wanted to do.

Although he was equally unsure that Luccy would actually come to his hotel later this evening. But if she considered him arrogant now, then she certainly wouldn't like his mood if he had to come looking for her a second time…

CHAPTER FOUR

'A VERY wise decision on your part,' Sin drawled as the lift doors of the penthouse suite opened to admit Luccy that evening. 'And only ten minutes late, too,' he added appreciatively as he stepped back to allow her to stride forcefully past him into the suite. 'I expected it to be eight o'clock at least before you put in an appearance,' he jeered as he followed her into the lounge.

A room that unfortunately brought back all too many memories for Luccy. Disturbing memories she had tried to forget, but couldn't...

She rounded on him fiercely. 'Let's just get this conversation over and done with, shall we?' she snapped, not at all happy with his absolute assurance that she would appear here some time this evening—just as he had told her she would.

But what else could she do when he seemed to know so much about her and she still didn't know what he was talking about half the time?

He raised dark brows. 'Are you sure you wouldn't like a glass of wine—or champagne—first, to help the evening along?'

Luccy speared him with a glare, knowing he was

enjoying mocking her by the amused glitter she could see in those silver eyes. 'This isn't an *evening*, it's a brief—very brief!—visit,' she announced, determined that she wouldn't acknowledge by so much as a glance that she was aware—and disturbed by!—how casually he was dressed this evening. His black tee shirt fitted tautly across the width of his shoulders and chest, and faded denims rested low down on his hips, his feet left bare.

'You don't mind if I go ahead?' He held up the bottle of white wine before pouring some into one of the two glasses he had waiting, and then taking a sip. 'It really is a very good Chablis,' he added temptingly. 'And I hate to drink alone.'

'This isn't a social call, either,' Luccy said tersely, aware that the suite had a more lived-in appearance this evening, a folded newspaper on the coffee table, some papers spread out on the desk near the window where he had obviously been busily working when she had arrived.

He was obviously a man who liked to work as hard as he played.

And, as Luccy knew only too well, he played extremely diligently!

'Pity,' Sin murmured huskily as he moved to sit down on the sofa, looking up at her as he rested the ankle of one foot on the other knee. 'You aren't here for the evening, and this isn't a social call, so what is it, Luccy?' he challenged softly.

'You're the one who insisted I come here tonight,' she reminded him. 'So why don't *you* tell me what it is?'

She looked stunningly beautiful again this evening, having changed the loose blouse and denims of earlier for a fitted apricot-coloured cashmere sweater that clung lovingly to the firm swell of her breasts, and tailored black trousers that emphasised the long length of her legs, a pair of strappy black high-heeled sandals adding to her height. That amazing blue-black hair was loose again tonight too and falling in a soft cascade over her shoulders and down the length of her spine.

Dressed to kill was the appropriate phrase, Sin believed, and Luccy was certainly looking lovely enough this evening to take his breath away...

Sin regarded her broodingly for several long seconds before answering her. 'Things were becoming a little—heated, at your studio earlier; I thought a cooling-off period might be beneficial.'

'For whom?' she asked.

'For both of us, as it happens,' he drawled. 'For goodness' sake sit down, Luccy,' he instructed irritably as he took another leisurely sip of his wine.

'I've already told you—I'm not staying!' She stubbornly continued to stand across the room.

Sin gave an impatient sigh. 'I don't intend staying long when I pay a visit to the dentist, but I do at least sit down!'

She grimaced. 'I'm glad you can see the similarity.'

Sin gave a shrug. 'I can see that from your point of view this may not be the most pleasant visit you've ever made, yes...'

She gave him a scathing glance. 'But not from yours?'

Of course he hadn't expected this to be a pleasant visit—how could it be when this woman had deliberately, calculatedly, made love with him three evenings ago. Just because he didn't look furious didn't mean that he wasn't!

Looking at Luccy from beneath hooded lids, he could see that she was just as angry...

Because she had been found out?

Whatever the reason, those deep blue eyes sparkled when she was angry, her cheeks became flushed, and her breasts strained against the soft material of her sweater. As for that blue-black hair! Just looking at its soft silkiness reminded him of how that long ebony swathe had fallen so enticingly about the nakedness of her shoulders the night they had made love together.

'No,' he bit out, 'I don't find being with you anywhere near as painful as a visit to the dentist.'

'It's early yet,' Luccy retorted swiftly.

'I have nothing else to do this evening—what about you?'

Luccy repressed a quiver down the length of her spine as she easily heard the underlying threat in his voice. 'Can we just get this over with?'

'By all means,' he agreed smoothly.

'Well?' Luccy prompted impatiently after at least a minute's silence had stretched between them.

He frowned darkly. 'I was giving you the opportunity to explain yourself.'

'How can I do that when I have no idea what you're talking about most of the time?' It had taken a tremendous effort of will on Luccy's part to come here this evening, the least this man could do was cooperate.

Sin's mouth thinned. 'I'd hoped the games would be over this evening.'

'Maybe they would be—if I knew what game we were playing!'

'I thought we had agreed it was blackmail—sorry, *leverage*?'

Luccy felt the heat in her cheeks. 'I still have no idea what you meant by that remark. As far as I can see, the only one guilty of using leverage is you—by forcing me to come here this evening!'

Sin's patience faded completely in the face of her continued claim of innocence. He hadn't expected this to be a pleasant evening, he was too coldly angry for that, but he would certainly have respected Luccy more if she could at least have been honest with him once she was found out.

'Okay, let's start with exactly when it was you realised who I am,' he growled.

Luccy eyed him blankly. 'Who you are?'

Sin gave an impatient sigh. Damn it, he didn't enjoy being made a fool of! 'I can see this is going to be a long evening, after all,' he rasped.

'No, it isn't,' she said. 'You tell me who you are, I'll go "wow", and then I can leave. Yes?'

'No,' Sin grated. 'But *Wow* is probably as good a place as any to start this conversation.'

Luccy became very still, her gaze wary now. 'You're referring to the magazine?'

His mouth tightened. 'I'm referring to one of its executives. Paul Bridger, to be exact, a man we both met—in my case, briefly—three evenings ago.'

Luccy nodded slowly. 'When he propositioned me and you interceded, yes.'

Resulting in Luccy having received a very politely worded letter the following day, from the secretary of Dale Harris, the other executive at that dinner meeting, informing her—surprise surprise!—that they had decided against contracting her to do any work for their magazine.

'I won't deny you gave a charming performance that night, but it really wasn't very fair on Paul Bridger,' Sin bit out disgustedly.

'Not *fair* on him?'

He nodded. 'You had already agreed to go to bed with him in exchange for being given a photographic assignment with the magazine he works for—'

'I most certainly had *not*!' Luccy glared at him indignantly, her hands clenching into fists at her sides.

'He says you did.'

'He—! When did you talk to him?' she demanded incredulously. '*Why* did you talk to him?'

Sin looked at her coldly. 'Let's just say I found the way you just disappeared the other evening while I was in the shower a little—questionable, to say the least—'

'It didn't occur to you that I might have been embarrassed by what had just happened between us?' she asked exasperatedly.

'No,' Sin said. 'But I was definitely curious enough to know that it might be in my best interest to—see you again. I had a little difficulty tracking you down at first,' he acknowledged ruefully, 'but enquiries at the hotel restaurant established that you had been dining with two executives from *Wow* magazine that evening. It wasn't too hard to find out the names of those executives, or to make an appointment to see the younger one—'

'You're incredible, do you know that?' Luccy gasped disbelievingly.

He gave an unapologetic shrug. 'I went along to Bridger's office this morning and had an illuminating little chat with him before coming to your studio.'

Luccy stared at him. Just stared at him. Sin had— Then he had— And he believed Paul Bridger's version of what had happened that night rather than her own? It was unbelievable! Absolutely unbelievable!

More than that, it was damned insulting!

'How very Sherlock Holmes of you!' she snapped.

'I thought so.' Sin's smile was completely lacking in humour.

She gave a disgusted shake of her head. 'And that night I thought you were—I believed—You're no better than Paul Bridger!'

His lips curled with distaste. 'Not a pleasant individual, I grant you. Although it wasn't exactly pleasant of you, either, to threaten him with the fact that he's married.'

'I didn't threaten him. You were there in the hallway. You heard some of what was said—'

'I heard you mention Bridger's wife,' he admitted grimly.

Luccy became very still. She had mentioned Paul's wife to him that evening. But only out of desperation, as a deterrent, not—

'He expected— He wanted— I only mentioned his wife because I was only trying to remind him of his— of his responsibilities,' she defended herself, realising just how lame that sounded.

'He claims you were trying to blackmail him into giving you work. His boss—Dale Harris is his name, I believe?—he seems to believe it too.'

This was a nightmare. An unbelievable nightmare. She had taken Paul and Dale to dinner, had paid for the whole damned evening—and now it seemed she was going to be made to pay in another way, too.

'Let me try and get this straight,' Luccy exclaimed. 'You believe I tried to blackmail Paul Bridger into giving me work on the magazine he works for by threatening to tell his wife that he tried to get me into bed after

our business meeting? You're also of the opinion, based
on that belief, that my ultimate intention was to somehow blackmail you, too?'

'That works for me, yes.' Sin nodded slowly. 'But
having transferred your attention onto me so impul-
sively it must have presented something of a problem
for you when I told you that I didn't have a wife, let
alone kids.'

Luccy frowned at his continued insistence that she
had deliberately planned what had happened between
them that evening. 'Even supposing—just supposing!—that your accusations were true, what do you
possibly have that I could want?'

'Off the top of my head?' he drawled derisively.
'Your future employment seems like a good enough incentive.'

Luccy had heard enough. She really had. 'What
future employment are you talking about?'

'You still have a contract with PAN Cosmetics, I
believe?'

Luccy became very still. He had mentioned the PAN
contract earlier today, too. As he had just mentioned her
future employment…

'What does any of that have to do with you?' she
asked warily.

Mocking brows rose over those icy grey eyes. 'Still
pretending ignorance, Luccy?'

She wasn't pretending at all! But she had a definite
premonition she wasn't going to like his answer when
it eventually came!

'Sleeping with the boss just isn't what it used to be,
is it?' he derided.

The boss? What boss?

The only boss Luccy had came with her contract with PAN Cosmetics...

She swallowed hard. 'You work for PAN Cosmetics?'

He gave an impatient sigh. 'I *own* PAN Cosmetics, Luccy. As you are well aware,' his voice grated harshly.

He owned...?

Luccy didn't just stare at him now—she goggled. 'Jacob Sinclair is head of Sinclair Industries, the company that owns PAN Cosmetics...' Was that strangulated voice really her own?

'Yes.'

Luccy could barely breathe now. 'But Jacob Sinclair is— Isn't he an elderly man, almost eighty?'

'Jacob Senior is eighty, yes,' Sin confirmed. 'He also stepped down as Chairman of Sinclair Industries almost ten years ago. As I'm sure you are well aware,' he added pointedly.

And why should she have known that? She worked exclusively with PAN Cosmetics, not Sinclair Industries.

Luccy could only stare at Sin as she waited for him to drop the next bombshell—one that she was sure was going to completely devastate her!

'Ordinarily, his son, Jacob Junior would have inherited that position, of course, but unfortunately Jacob Junior was killed in a car accident ten years ago.' His eyes were cold as he looked at Luccy.

Luccy moistened suddenly dry lips. 'So who did take over as chairman?'

Sin gave a weary sigh. 'Do we really have to continue with this act of ignorance on your part?'

'Just humour me, will you?' she rasped, totally agitated as he continued to play with her.

His mouth tightened. 'Jacob Sinclair the Third, Jacob

Senior's only grandchild now controls all the companies under ownership by Sinclair Industries. Which, of course, includes PAN Cosmetics.'

Luccy's eyes widened as the truth suddenly hit her with the force of a blow to the chest. *'You?'*

'Me.' He gave an unpleasant smile.

Him. He was Jacob Sinclair the Third. The grandson—and the only grandchild!—of Jacob Sinclair Senior.

The man who had become Luccy's lover three days ago...

The man who now believed—with the help of that lying louse Paul Bridger!—that she had deliberately transferred her attentions to him that evening because she had spotted a bigger fish to fry.

Her cheeks burned. 'I didn't know!' she gasped weakly. 'How could I possibly have known when you introduced yourself to me only as Sin that night?' she added accusingly.

'You introduced yourself only as Luccy, remember?'

'That was because—because—'

'Because you had recognised me in the restaurant earlier but didn't want me to know who you were!' A nerve pulsed in his tightly clenched jaw.

If Luccy had recognized this man as Jacob Sinclair three evenings ago, in the restaurant or anywhere else, then they wouldn't even be having this conversation!

Not that it mattered now. This man owned and ran Sinclair Industries, and consequently owned PAN Cosmetics, too.

The same man who was going to ensure that Lucinda Harper-O'Neill never worked for PAN Cosmetics again. Or possibly anyone else, either?

'Don't look so downcast, Luccy,' he jeered. 'You

aren't the first woman to use her body in order to try to get what she wants.' His mouth tightened.

Luccy stared at him. 'This— Are you saying that something like that has happened to you before?'

'Just the once,' he growled, the coldness of his expression telling her that it was not a pleasant memory—for him or the woman involved!

She swallowed hard. 'What happened…?'

His eyes narrowed to steely slits. 'Just a lowly employee of Sinclair Industries who thought she would like a promotion.'

'And she went to bed with you to get it?'

His face darkened ominously. 'Luccy—'

'What happened to her?' Luccy persisted.

He shrugged. 'After her employment was terminated? I have absolutely no idea.' His eyes glittered angrily.

Luccy gulped. 'I think I would like that glass of wine now,' she said shakily.

'I don't believe getting drunk is the answer to your problems,' Sin drawled mockingly even as he stood up to pour wine into the second glass before handing it to her.

Luccy ignored the comment, her hand trembling slightly as she took the glass from him. 'So.' She drew in a shaky breath after taking a sip of the chilled wine. 'Where do we go from here?'

'Where do you want us to go?'

Luccy looked up at him warily, seeing him for exactly what he was now. Not only the billionaire chairman of Sinclair Industries, but also a hard, powerful, and ruthless man. 'What do you mean?'

He grimaced. 'Well, obviously I have now made it clear to you that any attempt on your part to use our past—relationship, shall we say, as leverage of any kind, in order to renew your contract with PAN, is out of the question...' He looked up as Luccy stood up abruptly, his expression one of hard challenge as she began to pace the room agitatedly.

Luccy made no attempt to disguise her dislike as she glared across the room at him. 'I can assure you I did *not*—and most definitely *still* do not—have any intention of ever discussing that evening again. With anyone!'

'I'm pleased to hear it.'

'And that includes you!' Luccy snapped as she saw Sin's derisive expression. 'It was a mistake—'

'It was certainly a serious tactical error on your part,' he agreed.

Luccy slammed her glass forcefully down onto the table, mildly surprised when it didn't instantly shatter. '*You* seduced *me* that evening—'

'I believe it was a mutual seduction,' he corrected harshly.

'If it was mutual then why are you bitching about it?' Luccy was beyond even attempting to keep this conversation polite. Why should she bother when Sin had done nothing but insult her since coming to her studio this morning?

Why was he bitching? Sin questioned himself suddenly.

Probably because, although it had been ten years since he had last been this gullible, Sin could still clearly remember the humiliation he had felt, the sheer fury, at knowing how naïve and stupid he had been.

So much so that he could cheerfully have wrung Luccy's neck right now.

He had found his conversation with Paul Bridger

this morning offensive, to say the least. The other man, once he'd realised the purpose of Sin's visit, becoming extremely insulting about Luccy as he talked of the way she had encouraged him to believe they would be going to bed together at the end of the evening. That those insults were obviously true, going on the part of their exchange Sin had overheard, had only made his own conversation with Bridger more unpleasant.

'Nothing else to say?' she challenged Sin scathingly now.

There were a lot of things Sin could have said. But he wasn't about to say any of them. 'I believe the next move is up to you.'

She scowled. 'Obviously you will be terminating my employment with PAN Cosmetics immediately—'

'No.'

She raised startled brows. 'No…?'

Sin gave her a scathing glance of his own. 'You have three months left to run on your present contract, I believe?'

She eyed him warily. 'Yes, so?'

He nodded. 'Then you will continue to fulfil your obligations to PAN Cosmetics for that amount of time.'

'That's very—surprising, of you,' Luccy said warily.

'It's business, Luccy,' Sin rasped.

'And once that contract is over you will make sure I never work again, is that it?' she asked.

He continued to look at her coldly for several long seconds. 'I haven't made my mind up about that yet.'

Luccy knew by the absolute implacability of his expression that there was no point in her continuing to proclaim her innocence; this man simply didn't believe her. 'Let me know when you have!' she retorted before marching in the direction of the lift.

'Where the hell are you going?'

'I'm leaving, of course.' She stabbed her finger on the button to open the lift doors.

Sin stood up. 'I don't believe we've finished talking yet—'

'I have,' she assured him grimly as she stepped into the lift, her eyes glittering as she turned to face him before the lift doors slowly closed.

Sin was scowling darkly as he listened to the lift descending, knowing that the conversation hadn't gone at all as he had thought it would.

The tears he was sure he had seen glittering in Luccy's eyes didn't make much sense to him, either...

CHAPTER FIVE

'CHAMPAGNE?'

Luccy didn't need to turn and face the owner of that silkily soft voice to know who it belonged to. It might have been eight weeks since she had last heard it, but, as she had guessed at the time, she hadn't succeeded in forgetting a single thing about Jacob 'Sin' Sinclair, least of all the silky seductiveness of his voice!

She had wondered about—and dreaded!—seeing him again at this glitzy party being given in the New York Sinclair hotel to celebrate the launch of PAN Cosmetics' new brand of lipstick. But, as she was the photographer for all the publicity shots that had blitzed the media for the last month, it would have looked distinctly odd if Luccy had refused her own invitation to attend. Especially as she had decided that this particular photography assignment for PAN Cosmetics was to be her last...

Which didn't make it any easier for her to break off her present conversation in order to turn and face Sin!

Despite the fact that the reception room in this New York hotel was full of the press, as well as the rich and famous, Sin had had absolutely no problem picking out

Lucinda Harper-O'Neill in the sparkling crush of people. For one thing it was impossible not to spot that distinctive long, blue-black hair. For another, she was looking beautiful again in red...

Had she deliberately worn red again this evening as a challenge to him for that night two months ago?

Whatever her reason for wearing it, there was no doubting that Luccy looked stunningly beautiful, her low-necked, sleeveless red gown a shimmering sparkle of sequins that hinted at her curves rather than clung to them, and revealing a long expanse of shapely legs, the red high-heeled shoes she wore adding an extra three inches to her height. Her long blue-black hair was loose again tonight and curling silkily down the length of her spine, the deep blue of her eyes emphasised by long, curling black lashes, a delicate blush to her cheeks, and the fullness of her lips once again glossed a deep, tempting red.

Sin had stood across the room watching her for several minutes before approaching and speaking to her, his body tensing as he watched her conversing with one of the male executives of PAN Cosmetics, her beautiful face animated, her blue eyes glowing, her cheeks satiny smooth, and those red-glossed lips full and smiling to reveal her small, even white teeth.

That the man she was talking to was totally captivated by her glowing beauty was more than obvious—if Darren Richards leant any closer over the bare expanse of her creamy breasts he was going to lose himself down the front of that glittering red gown!

Sin turned his hard silver gaze on the older man. 'Richards,' he greeted tersely. 'I believe my grandfather was looking for you a few minutes ago...' he added pointedly.

Luccy, having turned to face Sin, barely noticed as Darren Richards excused himself and hurried away, her attention all on Sin. He looked tall, dark, and breathtakingly handsome in the black evening suit and snowy white shirt and bow tie, the expression in those silver-grey eyes totally unreadable as he coolly returned her gaze, holding out one of the two champagne glasses he carried.

'I won't, if you don't mind.' She shook her head as she held up her glass of sparkling water.

'Fine.' He shrugged before disposing of one of the glasses on the tray of a passing waiter. 'Have you been working your brand of magic on one of the PAN executives this time?'

Luccy had decided before coming to New York that if she and Sin did meet again she would not allow him to get under her skin. 'Do you think I succeeded?' she came back dryly.

Once again Sin couldn't help but admire her easy confidence. 'Judging by the way Darren almost fell into your cleavage? I would say that's a yes,' he confirmed mockingly. 'The only problem is, Darren doesn't have the final word over any future contracts you may or may not have with PAN.'

Luccy met his gaze unblinkingly. 'But you do?'

'Of course.' He gave a derisive inclination of his head.

'Pity.' She gave him a sweeping glance before turning her attention to the rest of the room. 'Did you say that your grandfather's here?'

Sin's mouth curved into a humourless smile. 'He may be eighty but he still makes a point of always appearing at these occasions. Would you like to meet him?'

'No, I don't think so, thank you,' she refused lightly.

'He doesn't bite,' Sin assured her dryly.

Unlike this man, that silver gaze warned Luccy!

'You don't want any champagne. You don't want to meet my grandfather. What *do* you want, Luccy?' he asked softly.

The huskiness of his voice caused a tingling at Luccy's nape and sent a quiver of awareness down the length of her spine, the bodice of her gown suddenly feeling too tight as her breasts swelled in response.

This man was playing with her, Luccy easily guessed, and he was enjoying doing it too!

'From you?' she bit out. 'I thought I had already made it clear at our last…meeting, that you don't have anything that I want.'

'I believe what you wanted was another contract with PAN?'

She looked at him coldly. 'There are plenty of other companies who have just as big an advertising budget, you know.'

'*Wow* and Paul Bridger came up trumps, after all, did they—?

'Where are you going?' Sin reached out to take a light hold of her arm as she would have walked away.

'Anywhere that you aren't,' she snapped. 'For your information, I haven't seen or spoken to Paul Bridger—or anyone that knows him,' she added pointedly, 'since talking to you at your hotel that evening. How about you?'

Sin raised a disdainful eyebrow. 'Why the hell would *I* want to see him?'

She shrugged those creamy shoulders as she looked at him challengingly. 'Oh, the two of you seemed to have *so* much in common.'

Insulting as well as courageous, Sin acknowledged

ruefully. Not that she had lacked courage the last time they had spoken, she just seemed different in some way. Or was it himself that was different? He'd had the same eight weeks to think of this woman and wonder if he really had been wrong about her, as Luccy had insisted so vehemently.

In the circumstances it was unfortunate that the first time he'd seen her this evening she had obviously been charming yet another executive, of PAN this time!

Luccy looked pointedly at the fingers that still encircled her arm. 'Take your hand off me, Sin,' she instructed softly. 'I'll give you three seconds and then I'm going to start screaming,' she added when he continued to frown down at her.

His mouth twisted. 'That would definitely make you the centre of attention!'

She raised dark brows. 'I believe that would bother you more than it would me.' After all, there were hundreds of members of the press present...

His eyes darkened with amusement as he slowly released her. 'Aren't you becoming a little—reckless, Luccy?'

'Am I?' She resisted the effort to rub the tingling spot on her arm where Sin's fingers had just touched her. 'Or maybe it's just that I don't care to be in the company of a man who has the opinion of me that you do,' she said sarcastically.

'And what opinion is that, Luccy?'

She gave a dismissive laugh. 'I don't believe I've ever met anyone else who has believed me capable of blackmail—let alone actually accused me of it!' Her voice had hardened over the last words, her eyes glittering angrily as she looked at him in furious challenge.

Sin's gaze was narrowed. 'You have to admit—'

'I *don't* have to admit anything, least of all to being guilty to any of the accusations you made against me,' Luccy insisted. 'And, fortunately, I don't have to stand here and hear them repeated, either. I find it rather warm in here, so if you'll excuse me—'

'No, Luccy, I won't *excuse you*,' Sin growled harshly as he stepped in front of her to stop her departure.

Sin wondered what it was about this particular woman that just touching the silky softness of her skin a few minutes ago had made him want to sweep her up in his arms and carry her out of here to the nearest bed.

None of the other women he had known had ever made him feel like shaking her and kissing her at the same time! In light of what had happened between them two months ago the first emotion was easily explained, but surely that second instinct should have been nullified by the first?

She eyed him coldly. 'What do you mean *no*?'

His mouth quirked humourlessly. 'Exactly what I said,' he grated tersely. 'I haven't finished talking to you yet—'

'But *I* have finished talking to *you*,' she announced calmly.

Sin looked about them impatiently; if anything the room was even more crowded and noisy than it had been a few minutes ago. 'Let's get out of here and go somewhere we can talk without interruption,' he rasped.

Luccy gave a disbelieving shake of her head. 'I'm not going anywhere with you, Sin.'

One thing she had decided on before she came to New York: if she did see Sin again then she certainly wasn't going to allow herself to be alone with him.

She only had to look at him now, at the lean ruthlessness of his face, the hard contours of his muscled body, to know that she was still as physically aware of him as she had been the night they'd met.

She only had to look at the hot glitter of Sin's eyes as he looked at her, the sensual twist to his lips, to know that he felt exactly the same way.

And it wasn't going to happen.

Not again.

Not ever.

He raised his eyebrows in tacit challenge. Then, 'Scared, Luccy?'

She flicked her hair back over her shoulder as her chin rose. 'That ploy may have worked once, Sin, but it isn't going to work a second time.'

Sin stood so he was barely inches away from her. 'How many times have you thought of our time together, Luccy? How many times have you lain awake in your bed at night aching with arousal?' he murmured.

Now that he was with Luccy again, practically touching her, Sin could recall each and every one of the nights he had lain awake in his own bed, hot and hard as he thought of the silky feel of this woman's skin, as he remembered surging into the heat of her tight sheath as she climaxed wildly and took him with her.

Unfortunately those memories had always quickly been followed by the realisation that she had only been using him that night...

How often had she thought of Sin Sinclair? Luccy asked herself achingly. Too many times, considering their last conversation! On several occasions she had even dreamt of this man, actually felt him inside her, only to awaken and find her body hot and trembling, her breasts full and tingling, a dampness between her thighs.

Had she come here tonight with the expectation of seeing Sin again? Had all her excuses, all the reasons she had given herself for having to be here, really been because she had needed to see Sin one last time? To know if that night two months ago had merely been an aberration on her part, or if she still wanted him?

Well, if she had, Luccy now had her answer—she trembled with the sheer physical awareness of just being near Sin again!

'I'm sorry to disappoint you, *Mr* Sinclair,' she told him scornfully, 'but I've been far too busy with my career to spare you a single thought.'

'Liar!'

Her eyes widened at his soft accusation. '*You—*'

'Are you going to keep this lovely young lady to yourself all evening, Sin?'

Luccy removed her gaze thankfully from Sin's glitteringly compelling one to look past him to the elderly man who had just joined them. He was tall and slender in the black evening clothes, with a shock of snowy-white hair, it was nevertheless easy to see from the similarity in the ruthless hardness of their features that this was Sin's grandfather, Jacob Sinclair Senior.

Her back stiffened as Sin moved to stand beside her and curve his arm lightly about her waist before making the introductions.

'Luccy, this is my grandfather, Jacob Sinclair,' he said smoothly. 'Grandfather, meet Lucinda Harper-O'Neill.'

Grey eyes almost as piercing as his grandson's looked her over speculatively. 'The clever young lady with the camera,' Jacob Sinclair finally murmured approvingly. 'You have done a tremendous job for us during this last year.'

Luccy raised surprised brows at his knowledge of her work. 'How nice of you to say so.'

'I don't believe that nice is necessarily a Sinclair trait, Miss Harper-O'Neill.' The elderly man chuckled. 'What do you say, Sin?' he prompted his grandson dryly.

'I say you could at least let Luccy get to know me a little better before telling her that,' Sin came back.

The elderly man gave an unrepentant grin. 'Our bark is much worse than our bite,' he confided in Luccy lightly.

Not in Luccy's experience, it wasn't!

Neither was she in the least comfortable with that possessive arm curved about her waist...

'What do you think, Luccy?' Sin felt, and ignored, Luccy's attempts to escape his hold on her waist, the tightening of his fingers warning her to cease her squirming. 'Is my bark worse than my bite?' he queried huskily, his mouth quirking mockingly as he saw the blush that now coloured her cheeks.

'Now, Sin, you really shouldn't embarrass Miss Harper-O'Neill in this way,' his grandfather admonished him laughingly.

'Please call me Luccy,' she invited the old man. 'And where your grandson is concerned, I do assure you I'm beyond feeling anything as mild as embarrassment.'

Sin felt his grandfather's briefly speculative gaze upon him, a gaze Sin met with cool deliberation. His grandfather might be eighty, but he was still one of the most astute men Sin had ever known. And Sin wasn't even attempting to conceal his interest in Luccy.

He had spent a lot of the last two months thinking about this woman. Two months when he'd had no interest in looking at another woman, let alone going to bed with one...

His grandfather was smiling as he turned back to Luccy. 'Perhaps you would care to accompany Sin to lunch at my home tomorrow?'

Luccy was no longer squirming in the curve of Sin's arm, but had become absolutely rigid as she looked at his grandfather. 'I don't think so, thank you, Mr Sinclair,' she said breathlessly. 'I'm hoping to be able to get an earlier flight back to England tomorrow.'

Sin's mouth compressed into a thin line. 'A sudden change of plans?'

'Very sudden,' she confirmed defiantly, those blue eyes flashing warningly as she turned to look up at him.

'See if you can't get her to change her mind, hmm, Sin?' his grandfather suggested speculatively. 'It was very nice to meet you, either way, Luccy,' he added warmly before taking his leave.

Luccy attempted once again to remove herself from the curve of Sin's arm as soon as the two of them were alone. This time she dug her nails into the back of his hand when he refused to release her, her gaze turning triumphant as he gave a pained wince before stepping away to look down at the crescent-shaped marks her nails had left in his skin.

He scowled. 'Now that definitely wasn't nice, Luccy.'

Luccy eyed him with satisfaction. 'I don't believe that *nice* is necessarily a Harper-O'Neill trait, either!'

He narrowed silver-grey eyes. 'My grandfather obviously wasn't a good influence on you.'

'Don't you think so?' she challenged brightly. 'I thought he was charming!'

'Unlike his grandson?'

'Oh, definitely,' she retorted sweetly.

Sin shook his head ruefully. 'Obviously the sentiment was reciprocated. My grandfather isn't in the habit of issuing luncheon invitations to every beautiful woman he meets,' he explained dryly at Luccy's questioning look.

Luccy was actually quite sorry that she hadn't been able to accept the older man's invitation. Surprisingly she had liked his forthright manner. But it really would be better if she went back to England as soon as possible.

Tonight had shown her irrefutably that the less she had to do with Sin, or his family, the better...

She turned away. 'I really do have to go and circulate now, Sin—'

'Where are you staying tonight?' he asked suddenly.

Luccy eyed him warily. 'Why do you want to know?'

Sin gave a humourless smile. 'I thought I might offer to see you back to your hotel later this evening.'

As Luccy was actually staying at *this* particular hotel he wouldn't have far to go!

But she had absolutely no intention of revealing that she had a suite booked on the fourth floor above them. As she had no intention of being alone anywhere with Sin, this evening or at any other time.

Coward, a little voice taunted inside her head.

Maybe. But she was too physically aware of Sin, remembered all too clearly where that physical attraction had taken her the last time they were alone in a hotel suite together, to want to tempt providence a second time.

Or herself!

'I wasn't intending to leave just yet,' she informed him. 'And even if I were, you would be the last person I would want to have take me back to my hotel!' she added insultingly.

Sin narrowed his gaze on her, knowing that the flush in her cheeks was no longer caused by anger, the blue of her eyes now mistily shimmering, her breasts swelling creamily over the scooped neckline of her gown.

Luccy was aroused by him.

As Sin was once again aroused by her.

And considering they were both consenting adults, with absolutely no illusions between them this time concerning their motives, he didn't see why the hell they shouldn't have each other if it was what they both wanted!

'Let's get out of here.' He firmly repeated his earlier suggestion.

'No.'

'Luccy.' Sin became very still as he looked down at her with glittering silver eyes. 'We can do this the hard way or the easy way. It's your choice.'

Luccy looked up at him searchingly, knowing by the tightness of his mouth and that angry glitter in his eyes that he meant what he said.

But she meant what she had said, too! 'Then it will have to be the hard way.' She faced him challengingly.

Sin's gaze narrowed on her speculatively for several long seconds, and whatever he saw there in her expression was enough to relax some of his tension. 'At this moment you want me as much as I want you,' he murmured confidently.

She could deny it, of course. But what would be the point…?

Instead she gave him a mocking smile. 'And does the spoilt little rich boy always get what he wants?'

'No.' His teeth showed in a humourless smile of his own. 'But Jacob Sinclair the Third does!'

'Really?' Luccy gave a softly derisive laugh. 'Then he's going to be awfully disappointed when he finally realises I've turned him down, isn't he?'

Sin really couldn't help but admire this woman. Almost as much as he desired her...

He quirked dark brows. 'You're leaving some time tomorrow, you said?'

'Yes, that's right,' she confirmed warily.

'I could always offer to fly you home on the Sinclair jet when you're ready to leave.'

'Is that supposed to impress me?' she scorned.

'It sure as hell impresses me every time I climb aboard it!'

'It's an indulgence I think I'll manage to forgo, thanks,' Luccy told him with saccharine sweetness.

This man—the Sinclair family, at least—owned their own jet!

She was way, way, way out of her depth...

She gave a bright meaningless smile as she prepared to leave. 'I'm sure I don't have to lie and say what a pleasure it's been to see you again?'

He grinned unconcernedly. 'The pleasure has been all mine, I assure you.'

'If you enjoy being with a woman who holds you in nothing but contempt, then, yes, it would appear so,' Luccy snapped.

His eyes narrowed dangerously, telling Luccy that she had probably gone too far with that last remark.

'If you won't have lunch with my grandfather

tomorrow perhaps you would have it with me, instead,' he bit out coldly.

Luccy's eyes widened. 'Why on earth would I want to do that?'

Sin shrugged. 'Perhaps because you would like to be the one given the photographic contract with PAN when it's reviewed next month?'

Luccy frowned. 'We both know that isn't going to happen.'

'Do we?'

Luccy looked at him searchingly, noting the challenge in his expression, the hard twist to his mouth. 'Yes,' she finally sighed. 'It's common gossip that Roy Bailey wants that contract.'

'What Bailey wants and what he gets could be two different things. I really do have the final say on who gets the contract, Luccy,' he said.

Luccy raised incredulous brows. 'Are you by any chance using *blackmail* into forcing me to have lunch with you tomorrow, Mr Sinclair?'

'I believe the word you prefer is *leverage*. And the answer to that is yes,' he confirmed unapologetically.

This man— He— *Ooh!* Luccy gritted her teeth to keep the words back. She could never remember feeling so frustratedly angry before! What she wanted to do was tell this man what he could do with his contract, but caution warned her that it would be better if she was on the other side of the Atlantic—well out of Sin's reach—when he learnt that she had already told Darren Richards she had no interest in signing another contract with PAN even if it was offered to her.

She flicked a look at him from beneath lowered eyelashes. 'What time do you want me and where?'

Sin didn't show by so much as a flicker of an eyelid that he was disappointed by her answer. Part of him had wanted—hoped—that Luccy would tell him what he could do with both his lunch and his contract.

Face it, Sin, he told himself derisively, Luccy really is only interested in what she can get from you. So much so that she would even agree to have lunch with you tomorrow.

'Here at one o'clock,' he rasped. 'The penthouse apartment at this hotel, like the one at The Harmony, is always available for family use,' he added mockingly as she raised questioning brows.

Providence was already working against her, Luccy acknowledged heavily. 'How convenient for you,' she drawled.

Sin bared his teeth in a humourless smile. 'It can be.'

Luccy would just bet that it could!

She had assumed, naïvely, that they would be having lunch in a restaurant, not in the privacy of another hotel suite.

Could she handle being alone with Sin again? Did she want to be alone with Sin again?

What choice did she have? Once she was back in England she would be safely out of his reach, but until that happened she had to go along with Sin's belief that she was still interested in renewing her contract with PAN. At any price, apparently!

'Very well,' she accepted briskly. 'But it will have to be a very brief lunch,' she added warningly. 'I really do intend getting on an earlier flight back to England tomorrow.'

'I'll make our—conversation, as brief as I can, Luccy,' Sin said dryly.

Luccy felt the colour warm her cheeks as she heard the innuendo beneath that statement.

If Sin thought she was going to bed with him tomorrow lunchtime then he was going to be very disappointed!

CHAPTER SIX

'DO TRY and lighten up, Luccy,' Sin murmured as Luccy, having refused his offer of a glass of the chilled white wine, now refused to sit down either but instead stood tensely across the sitting-room of the penthouse suite of the Sinclair Hotel. 'Maybe if we attempted a little polite conversation?'

'Is that even possible?' She shot him a scathing glance, her appearance very businesslike in a white silk blouse and fitted black trousers, her hair secured in a neat chignon.

'I don't see why not,' Sin said lightly as he sat down on the cream sofa. 'Tell me about your family. Do you have siblings? Parents?'

'Well, of course I have parents, Sin,' she came back sarcastically.

His mouth tightened. 'I meant ones that are still alive.'

Luccy sighed impatiently. 'Yes, I have a mother and father, both still living, and whom I love very much. I also have a sister, Abby. She's going through a very messy divorce at the moment,' she added with a frown.

'That's a pity.' Sin also frowned. 'Any children involved?'

'Two.' Luccy nodded.

'Even more of a pity,' he sympathised.

'I think so, yes,' Luccy said abruptly.

Her sister Abby's eight-year marriage had been a disaster almost from the beginning, and was one of the reasons that Luccy had always steered shy of relationships herself. The main reason, in fact.

Abby had been eighteen and three months pregnant with Alice when she and Rory had married so hastily. But it had been obvious within weeks of Alice being born that Abby and Rory should never have married each other, the attraction that had been between them when they had first met, and which had resulted in Abby's pregnancy, having very quickly turned to resentment on Rory's part and discontent on Abby's. But instead of ending the marriage as they should have done, Abby and Rory had added to the mess by having Josh just a year after Alice had been born.

After eight years of unhappiness the two of them had finally decided to admit defeat and get a divorce. But even that had turned into a battleground as they wrangled, not just over the children, but the house and everything in it.

Not a shining example of marital bliss for Luccy to want to emulate any time soon!

'What about you, Sin?' she queried. 'I know you don't have any siblings, but you mentioned your mother is still alive…?'

He nodded. 'She moved back to her beloved Savannah after my father died, but she comes back to New York on a regular basis.' The affection could be heard in his voice. 'She—ah, I believe our lunch has arrived.' He stood up to answer the knock on the door. 'I took the liberty of ordering for both of us. I hope you don't mind.'

Luccy didn't mind in the least—as long as Sin didn't question the fact that she might not be able to eat what he had ordered!

She could smell the fish before Sin had even removed the domed silver covers from the plates, her stomach instantly churning in rebellion, feeling the slight sheen of perspiration that appeared on her top lip even as she fought back that nausea.

She lost that particular battle as soon as she looked at the medley of fish laid out so beautifully on the plates. 'Bathroom!' she choked weakly.

Sin looked up in astonishment. 'What?'

'Bathroom!' Luccy repeated desperately. 'Now! Unless you want me to be ill all over the carpet!'

'Second door on the left,' Sin told her slightly dazedly, staring after her in consternation as she made a mad dash down the hallway.

What the hell was going on?

'When were you going to tell me?' Sin demanded harshly several minutes later when Luccy returned to the sitting-room, her face deathly white.

Luccy stared at him as he stood across the room so broodingly tall and seething with explosive anger.

She moistened dry lips. 'Tell you what?'

'I advise you against treating me like a fool, Luccy,' he warned coldly.

'Heaven forbid anyone should do that!' She shook her head, determined not to be cowed by the ruthless expression on his face, or the dangerous glitter in those arctic grey eyes. 'But I'm really not sure what you want me to say—'

'I really do advise you to stop right there, Luccy!'

he said in a carefully controlled voice. 'Do *not* compound the seriousness of this situation by lying about the reason you were ill!'

Luccy swallowed hard. Sin couldn't know. He might suspect, but he couldn't actually know!

'I must have eaten something that disagreed with me,' she dismissed lightly. 'Probably one of the canapés last night. But I'm fine now,' she said reassuringly.

Sin's hands clenched at his sides, and his teeth were clamped together so tightly that his jaw actually ached, both in an effort to hold onto his temper. He rarely, if ever, lost control, his anger tending to take the form of icy deliberation rather than a fiery explosion.

But this woman was seriously in danger of pushing him beyond that icy control. He very much doubted that she would like the result if that were to happen!

'You're telling me that's the reason you were ill just now?'

'Of course.'

'I don't believe you,' he growled.

She gave an unconcerned shrug. 'That's your prerogative, I suppose.'

Sin looked at her searchingly, easily noting the changes in her now that he knew what he was looking for: there were dark shadows beneath those bewitching blue eyes that indicated a lack of sleep, her cheeks were more hollow than they had been, and there were lines of tension beside her unsmiling mouth.

His gaze moved lower. She was still incredibly slender, but he was sure that her breasts were slightly fuller than he remembered...

He wasn't wrong in his conclusion, Sin was sure that he wasn't!

He had spent the time while Luccy was in the bathroom considering all the options—including that she might have eaten something that disagreed with her. But the more obvious reason for her sudden nausea was the one that refused to go away...

'When were you going to tell me, Luccy?' he insisted.

Her chin rose. 'Tell you what?'

Sin forced himself to relax. Losing his temper really wasn't going to help this situation. 'Okay, Luccy, let's try getting to the truth another way, shall we?'

'I've already told you the truth. I obviously ate something last night that disagreed with me—'

'Why did you refuse to drink any champagne last night?'

He couldn't know, Luccy reminded herself again firmly. Sin absolutely could not know!

'I never drink alcohol when I'm working,' she explained calmly. 'Last night may have been a party, but it was still work as far as I'm concerned,' she added.

'You refused wine just now, too,' he pointed out flatly.

'I'm flying home later today—'

'Luccy,' Sin cut in warningly. 'While you were in the bathroom just now I did a little thinking.' A lot of thinking, actually. And his conclusion had left him almost paralysed with shock.

She drew in a ragged breath. 'I think it's time I was going—'

'Sit down!' he barked.

Her eyes flashed deeply blue as she glared at him. 'How dare you tell me what to do?'

Sin's mouth twisted impatiently as he crossed the

room to stand in front of her. 'Oh, I think you'll find I dare a lot more than that, Luccy. For the last time, *when* were you going to tell me?'

He was extremely intimidating standing close to her like this, fury etched into his arrogantly handsome face, a warning in the glitter of his eyes.

Luccy broke the intensity of that gaze to turn away. 'I have a plane to catch—'

'You won't be going anywhere today.'

Luccy became very still as she slowly turned back to face him, her eyes wide as she looked at him warily.

Sin's face was hard, implacable, those silver eyes shimmering like shards of ice, his shoulders stiff and unyielding, the muscles in his arms tensed. Like a huge jungle cat poised to pounce!

She moistened dry lips. 'Of course I'm going back to England today—'

'No, you're not,' Sin bit out evenly.

'You have no right to dictate where I do or don't go—'

'Luccy, I am holding onto my temper by a very slim thread.' His voice was low and menacing. 'I don't want to have to shake the truth out of you, but, believe me, if I have to, I will!'

One look at the grimness of Sin's expression was enough to tell her that he meant every word that he said.

Luccy could feel herself trembling, her legs beginning to shake, so much so that she stumbled towards one of the chairs and sat down heavily to look up at Sin with huge, haunted blue eyes.

Sin wasn't enjoying this conversation one little bit, especially now that he could clearly see the effect it was having on Luccy. But he had no intention of letting her just walk out of here, either. Not now. Not ever!

He continued to look at her, his gaze compelling her to answer.

She closed her eyes briefly before opening them again, her gaze challenging. 'I'm pregnant, Sin,' she murmured softly. 'Eight weeks pregnant, to be exact,' she added defiantly. 'But, then, you had already guessed that, hadn't you?' she concluded self-derisively.

Having his suspicions and having those suspicions confirmed were two totally different things, Sin discovered. Now he was filled with a whole new set of emotions. Awe, firstly, at the knowledge that Luccy carried his child. Tenderness, at the thought of the child, his child, growing inside her. Quickly followed by a return of anger as he wondered exactly when Luccy had intended telling him!

No, for the moment Sin wouldn't go there. If he thought about that now, then anger would become his prime emotion, and even if that anger was perfectly justified it certainly wasn't going to help an already fraught situation.

Instead he opted for being cool and controlled. 'Have you seen a doctor?' he prompted as he slowly turned to face her.

Luccy looked at him frowningly for several seconds before answering. 'Yes.' She nodded. 'The baby's fine. I'm fine.' She shrugged. 'He doesn't foresee any complications.'

To say that she was surprised at Sin's relative calm following her announcement would be a big understatement! He had to know, by the fact that she had stated so clearly that she was eight weeks pregnant, that the baby was his.

Not that it could ever have been anyone else's—no

matter what Sin might choose to believe to the contrary. The last—and only—time that Luccy had been in an intimate relationship had been seven years ago.

How did he really feel, now Luccy had confirmed that she was carrying his baby? She could discern absolutely none of Sin's emotions from looking at him, his expression closed as he continued to look at her with those enigmatic grey eyes.

But surely he had to feel something on hearing he was to become a father?

Didn't he…?

Personally, Luccy had been absolutely dumbstruck when the doctor had announced that the symptoms that had brought her to his clinic in the first place—tiredness, nausea, lack of appetite, a late period—could all be attributed to the fact that she was pregnant.

Pregnancy simply hadn't occurred to her as an explanation for those symptoms!

Why it hadn't, she had no idea. Probably because she stupidly hadn't thought that a single evening of unprotected lovemaking—unprotected because Luccy simply hadn't thought she would actually be making love with Sin or, indeed, anyone else that night!—could have resulted in her becoming pregnant.

'That's good,' Sin answered evenly, still determined to keep this situation from spilling over into anger if at all possible. 'Very good,' he repeated. 'Although I'll obviously want you to see someone over here as soon as possible—'

'Why will you?' she questioned sharply.

He raised a dark brow. 'Luccy, I'm sure your own doctor is a more than capable GP, but I would obviously prefer you to see a specialist of my choosing—'

'Maybe we should get something straight right now, Sin,' she cut in determinedly as she stood up. 'This is my baby, and—'

'And mine,' he grated harshly.

'Yes.' She nodded abruptly. 'But it will be up to *me* to decide which doctor I see during my pregnancy.'

His mouth twisted. 'I think we both know that isn't true.'

Luccy became very still as she looked at him warily. 'What do you mean?'

Sin turned away to thrust his hands into the pockets of his jeans. Before he reached out and touched Luccy again. Something that would be a definite mistake on his part.

Luccy was pregnant.

With his baby.

And ordinarily that would be reason for celebration—it *was* reason for celebration! Sin just had no idea yet what Luccy intended doing about it…

'Sin…?'

His face was an expressionless mask as he turned back to face her.

'The child you're carrying is the Sinclair heir.'

'What if it's a girl?' she came back challengingly.

'I already told you I'm the only grandson, so, girl or boy, as soon as it's born, this child will automatically become the Sinclair heir,' he bit out tersely. 'I'm sure you aren't unaware of what that means?'

Luccy had a sinking feeling she really wasn't going to like the rest of this conversation! Not that it had been exactly enjoyable so far, but the way this was going she just knew it was going to get worse…

She frowned. 'All it means to me is that my child's father is named Jacob Sinclair the Third.'

'Our child will be the Sinclair heir!'

'So you've said. Repeatedly.' Luccy grimaced. 'But that will only apply until you have other, legitimate children—'

'What makes you so sure that I don't intend for this child be legitimate?' Sin cut in forcefully, those grey eyes once again glittering arctically.

Luccy gave him a bewildered look. The only way the child she carried could be legitimate was if— 'You can't seriously think I want to *marry* you?' She gasped incredulously.

He gave a pitying glance. 'I'm sure that you would much rather I set you up in your own home and kept you and our child in the life to which you no doubt long to become accustomed—' He broke off as Luccy's hand swung up in an arc and made sharp contact with his cheek. 'Feeling better?' he taunted, the marks of her fingers already showing on his tightly clenched cheek.

'Not particularly, no!' She glared up at him, so angry that she was shaking with the emotion. 'I dislike you intensely!'

'So you've said. Repeatedly.' He gave a mocking inclination of his head. 'I can assure you, I'm not particularly fond of you at the moment, either. Not a prestigious start to a marriage, is it?'

'I am *not* marrying you!' Luccy repeated furiously.

Sin gave a humourless smile. 'I think you'll find that's exactly what you're going to do.'

'No—'

'It isn't something that's up for negotiation, Luccy,' he cut in grimly. 'Marriage is my price,' he declared.

'Are you *deaf*? I've just told you that I don't want to marry you!' she all but shrieked in frustration.

He shrugged. 'Maybe that was something you should have thought about before you became pregnant.'

Luccy gasped. 'You don't think I became pregnant on purpose?'

'I'll admit it had to have been more luck than judgement.' Sin shrugged. 'You just got *very* lucky.'

He couldn't seriously believe that Luccy had planned this pregnancy?

But he did. Luccy could see by the utter ruthlessness of his expression that that was exactly what Sin thought.

She was barely used to the idea of being pregnant herself, so to have Sin now accuse her of having planned it that way was incredible!

'People don't get married nowadays just because the woman is pregnant!' she protested.

Sin looked down at her coldly. 'I do.'

'So did my sister,' Luccy reminded him. 'That's the reason that eight unhappy years and two children later she's in the middle of a messy divorce!'

And Luccy didn't want that for herself or her child. She couldn't believe that Sin really wanted to be married to a woman he didn't love, either…

She gave a heavy sigh. 'Sin, I'm twenty-eight years old, and quite capable of bringing this child up on my own. I certainly don't intend marrying any man—even a Sinclair!—just because I happen to be expecting his baby.'

'Luccy, you may as well get used to the idea that there is no question of your bringing this baby up on your own.'

'Why isn't there?'

His mouth twisted. 'I've already explained the reasons why. Repeatedly, remember?' he drawled. 'There is an alternative, of course. One I'm sure you must have considered…'

Luccy frowned, not knowing what he meant. Then…'I have *not*, and I *will not*, consider having an abortion!' she told him forcefully.

'I'm glad to hear it,' Sin rasped, 'but that wasn't the alternative I was referring to. Are you willing to hand the baby over to me after it's born? In exchange for a cash settlement, of course?' His top lip curled back with distaste.

Luccy recoiled as if he had struck her, even more taken aback by this suggestion than she had been by his earlier one. Sin wanted to take the baby away from her…? Wanted to give her money in exchange for handing her baby over to him after it was born?

Until that moment Luccy hadn't been sure herself how she felt about her pregnancy—she had still been in a state of shock from learning she was pregnant at all!

Mostly she had ignored it, deciding it was something she could deal with later, when it became more of a reality.

But Sin's suggestion that he take the baby from her after it was born suddenly made it very real to her. She was expecting a baby. Her baby. Admittedly it was Sin's baby too, but even so—!

'No way,' she told him fiercely even as her hands moved protectively over her stomach where her baby nestled safe and warm. 'Absolutely *no way*!' She glared at him.

Sin, having half prepared himself to hear Luccy say she would accept his offer, now felt the relief wash over him at the fierceness of her refusal.

Maybe there was hope for the two of them yet…

CHAPTER SEVEN

'It's settled, then.' Sin nodded decisively. 'We're getting married.'

'The fact that *you* have made a decision does not make it settled, Sin!' Luccy told him exasperatedly. 'You have just insulted me in the worst possible way, seem to think that I deliberately planned this pregnancy for mercenary reasons, and now you calmly assume we're getting married!' She gave a determined shake of her head. 'I don't think so, Sin.'

He gave a rueful shrug. 'Do you have any other suggestions—viable ones,' he added harshly as Luccy would have spoken.

'My having the baby and continuing to live and work in London *is* a viable suggestion.'

'Not to me.'

Luccy felt as if she were going round and round in ever-decreasing circles—with no way out of the labyrinth! 'People—even pregnant ones—who take a big step like marrying each other should be in love when they do.'

'Who's to say that we won't learn to love each other, given time?'

'I somehow doubt that very much!' Luccy muttered.

Sin shrugged. 'Stranger things have happened.'

'Not to me, they haven't!' she growled.

'In that case, as I fully intend for us to be married before the baby is born, it would appear I have seven months in which to convince you otherwise, doesn't it?' he pointed out. 'I'll try to make those months as pleasurable for both of us as possible.'

'If you think you can seduce me into falling in love with you, then all I can say is you must have a very inflated opinion of the effect your lovemaking has on me!' Luccy was breathing hard in her agitation.

Sin slowly crossed the room, his movements all feline stalking. 'I'll probably have to work pretty hard at it,' he acknowledged dryly. 'But as I said, I'll endeavour to make sure that you enjoy the experience...' He stood in front of her now, those grey eyes gleaming like molten steel as he looked down at her.

Sin's eyes were like heated mercury, Luccy thought inconsequentially as she found herself unable to look away from the warmth of that gaze as it moved slowly over her slightly flushed features. And just as lethal if she got too physically close!

If Sin set out to deliberately break down her defences, then she wouldn't stand a chance. She gave a determined shake of her head as she tried to evade the spell that heated gaze was weaving about her senses. 'I have a plane to catch—'

'Not today, I'm afraid, Luccy,' Sin told her softly.

'I've already warned you not to presume to tell me what I can and can't do, Sin,' she retorted.

He didn't bother to reply as he moved to pick up the telephone receiver before pressing a single button. 'Reception?' His gaze held Luccy's as he spoke into the mouthpiece. 'Could you call the airport and cancel Miss Harper-O'Neill's flight to England later today? Thanks,' he added decisively before replacing the receiver to look at her challengingly.

'Damn it! I'll simply rebook!' Luccy told him with angry impatience. 'You really are the most arrogant man it has ever been my misfortune to meet!' She glared at him.

'Was meeting me really so unfortunate, Luccy?' he prompted huskily even as he reached out and curved his hand about her cheek before running the pad of his thumb caressingly across her bottom lip.

A caress Luccy felt from the hair on top of her head to the skin on the soles of her feet as it completely eradicated every other thought in her head.

Her lips tingled from the caress, the whole of her body becoming sensitised, breasts firming, nipples tightening, a warm clenching sensation in the pit of her stomach, that familiar heat between her thighs.

Luccy was still furious with Sin for the insulting remarks he had made to her earlier. Even more so for his high-handedness in cancelling her flight just now.

Obviously, just not furious enough to prevent herself from physically responding to him…

Before meeting Sin she had never thought of herself as a particularly sensual person, hadn't found her previous physical experience particularly stimulating, and had only mildly enjoyed the few kisses she had received at the end of other dates over the years. Yet Sin only had to look at her in a certain way, to touch her however lightly, and she felt that caress all the way from her head down to her toes.

'Was it, Luccy?' Sin persisted huskily, the lure of her parted lips proving almost too much of a temptation to him as he touched their softness, his whole body having tensed with awareness.

She swallowed hard. 'Can you doubt it when it's resulted in an unwanted pregnancy?'

Her breath was like a light caress across the tops of his fingers, totally distracting him from the sting of her words. 'It isn't unwanted by me.'

Her eyes widened. 'How can you say that when you're insisting on marrying a woman you don't even like?'

'Who says I don't like you?'

Luccy stared up at him exasperatedly. 'Of course you don't like me! You can't possibly like someone you don't trust.'

Sin didn't answer her in words, his hand dropping back to his side before he slowly lowered his head and captured her lips with his own, not touching her in any other way now as he sipped and tasted their pouting softness and he felt her quiver in response beneath the gentle onslaught.

Sin knew when a woman responded to his kisses. Just as he knew that Luccy's response to him the night they had made love had been completely genuine. As had his own response to her.

Even if they never felt more for each other than that physical desire, surely, for the sake of their child, it would be enough to sustain a marriage?

Sin raised his head slightly to look directly into the dark blue of her eyes. 'Now do you believe me when I say I don't dislike you?' he prompted gruffly.

Luccy didn't know what to believe any more!

But she couldn't marry a man who didn't love her just because he physically aroused her every time he so much as touched her. That sort of heated passion didn't last, and once that had died what would they have left? The same disastrous mess as Abby and Rory's marriage had been.

She drew in a ragged breath. 'I believe that at the moment, because of the baby, you think that marriage is what you want,' she conceded huskily. 'But—' Sin placed silencing fingertips over her lips.

'I want our baby to grow up with two parents, Luccy,' he told her emotionally. 'The same way that I did. The same way that you did.'

'And once this baby has grown up, where would that leave the two of us?'

'As grandparents, possibly?'

He really was serious about her marrying him!

It was tempting, oh-so-tempting, to accept his offer of marriage and to hell with what happened later. To lay down the mantle of responsibility and let Sin take charge.

But even for the sake of the baby she carried Luccy knew that without that magic ingredient of a shared love—something Sin would never, ever feel for her!— they didn't stand a chance of making a marriage between them succeed.

Sin had watched the flickering emotions on Luccy's expressive face, had seen that brief flare of doubt quickly followed by one of firm resolve. 'Let's just forget about the whole idea of marriage for the moment and concentrate on getting to know each other, instead,' he suggested. 'I doubt it's good for you, or the baby, if you continue to upset yourself in this way.'

'You aren't going to be one of those overprotective prospective fathers who attempts to wrap the pregnant woman in cotton wool until after the birth, are you?' she challenged. 'Because if you are I think I should tell you right now that I'm pregnant, not ill. I also intend to continue working until the moment they wheel me into the delivery-room!' Her eyes sparkled like twin sapphires as she glared at him rebelliously.

'Sinclair wives don't work,' Sin told her arrogantly. 'And especially not when they're pregnant,' he added firmly.

'This one will!'

Sin knew that there would have to be a lot of adjusting, by both of them, over the next seven months and beyond, but he was determined not to be goaded into arguing with Luccy before they had even begun.

He took a deep breath. 'If you insist, I'll just come along and carry your equipment for you.'

Luccy eyed him frustratedly. 'Sin, I don't think you're taking what I have to say seriously.'

'Sure I am,' he said briskly. 'Is your luggage downstairs in your room?'

'How did you know—? How long have you known it was this hotel I've been staying at?'

Sin's smile was wicked. 'I made it my business to know once I realised you couldn't be relied upon to keep our luncheon appointment. Reception had strict instructions to let me know if you tried to book out.'

Luccy should have known. He was a Sinclair, after all. Besides, he owned the damned hotel!

'Your luggage, Luccy?' he prompted.

'Yes, of course it's in my room, ready for when I book out,' she said. 'But—where are we going?' she demanded as he opened the door out into the corridor before waiting for her to precede him out of the suite.

'First to get your luggage, and then home,' he informed her.

'Home?' she echoed sharply, her eyes widening. '*Your* home?'

'Well, of course my home,' Sin said.

'But—I thought—'

'Yes?'

She shook her head. 'I thought you lived here…'

'In a hotel?' Sin raised dark brows. 'Hardly.'

Luccy still hung back. 'You don't live with your grandfather, do you?'

Luccy had been apprehensive and, yes, a little scared, when only she knew of her pregnancy, as she'd wondered how she was going to continue working once the baby was born, amongst other things. But having Sin just step in and take over in this way was even more frustrating. She certainly didn't intend going to stay with his grandfather!

Sin shot her a mocking glance. 'I'm thirty-five, Luccy, not five! I've had my own home for fifteen years or so,' he added dryly.

Luccy continued to protest at Sin's high-handedness even as she followed him down to her room, scowling at him as he stood to one side to allow her to unlock the door.

'This is unbelievable,' she complained, having no choice but to continue following him as he strode off to the lift with her two bags. One of them only had her clothes in, but the other one contained her camera and other equipment, expensive equipment she wasn't willing to let out of her sight. 'You can't just kidnap someone against their will!' she muttered even as she stepped into the lift beside him.

Sin glanced at her. 'I'm not kidnapping you, Luccy—I'm kidnapping your camera!' he teased.

Her eyes narrowed in warning. 'I could always call the police.'

'And tell them what, precisely? That I've stolen your camera? Yeah, they're really going to believe that!' Sin gave her an evil grin.

Of course the police wouldn't believe her if she said Sin had stolen her camera and equipment; Sin was rich enough to buy himself a thousand—a million!—cameras like hers. She doubted the accusation of kidnapping would be believed, either...

This really was incredible.

Unbelievable.

And, Luccy realised belatedly, completely inevitable the moment Sin had known that she was pregnant with his baby...

'I know we have some tea bags somewhere,' Sin muttered with his head in one of the kitchen cupboards.

The meticulously clean and tidy kitchen cupboards. In fact, the whole house was so neat and tidy that Luccy felt she should have taken her shoes off before she entered.

She had been more than a little surprised when, instead of driving to some luxurious penthouse apartment in Manhattan, Sin had driven his foreign sports car out of New York completely and into the suburbs to this rambling single-storey ranch-style house surrounded by its own acres of forest and parkland set behind a high wall and huge iron security gates.

The inside of the house was even more surprising, the hallway alone big enough to be one of the rooms in her own London flat.

There were pale cream marble floors and comfortable brocade furniture throughout the whole of the house as Luccy followed Sin through to the kitchen. The paintings on the walls were obviously originals—even the Monet—and the huge kitchen itself was like something out of a glossy magazine, with its green and cream tiled floor, cream units, an array of copper pans suspended along one wall, and a huge picture window at one end that looked out over the forest and rolling parkland.

Luccy stood hesitantly in the doorway. 'Do you live here alone?' It was a very large house for one man.

Ideal for a family, of course, and an ideal setting in which to bring up a child...

Sin straightened to look at her knowingly. 'There's no other woman in residence, if that's what you're asking,' he drawled. 'Nor has there ever been,' he added as she didn't look convinced.

'Is it always this neat and tidy?' Luccy grimaced as she stepped tentatively onto the cream and green tiled floor.

Sin took the tea bags from the cupboard then looked about the kitchen. He rarely came in here as it happened, but he could see now that the copper pots shone along one wall, with not a single item left out on the green marble work surfaces to spoil its neat symmetry, the cream wood units gleaming spotlessly.

He turned back to her with a frown. 'You don't like neat and tidy?'

'Well...yes, of course I *like* neat and tidy,' she protested. 'It's just that I'm notoriously the opposite.'

Ah, she was looking for reasons as to why the two of them would never be able to live together...

'No problem.' Sin shrugged as he took a cereal packet from one of the cupboards and scattered its contents over one of the worktops before taking a carton of milk from the fridge and tipping that on top of the cereal. 'I can drop an egg or two on the floor too if that would make you feel more comfortable?' He quirked dark brows.

'I said I was untidy, not a slob!' Luccy gave him an exasperated glare even as she moved to pick up a cloth and clean up the mess he had made.

Sin leant back against one of the units as he watched her. 'Would you like to see the study where I work when I'm at home?' he offered once she had cleaned up to her satisfaction.

She eyed him warily. 'Is that some sort of obscure sexual invitation? Like another man asking me if I would like to see his etchings or even the family jewels?'

Having Luccy as a possible constant in his life was already turning out to be a lot more enjoyable than Sin had expected. He had already accepted that he was deeply sexually attracted to her, as he knew she was to him, and he had certainly never been bored in her company to date, but somehow he hadn't expected to have fun with her, too...

'And if it were a sexual invitation...?'

'I would tell you I've already seen them!'

Sin found himself grinning at her waspish tone. 'No doubt you will see them again, too.'

She eyed him challengingly. 'You think so?'

'I live in hopes of that being the case, yes,' he said wryly. 'But my invitation to come and look at my study was exactly that,' he continued briskly as he saw a light of rebellion creeping back into those incredible blue eyes.

He had done very well by succeeding in getting her to the house in the first place without too much resistance on her part—he certainly didn't want to push his luck.

Luccy frowned her puzzlement. 'And why would I want to see your study?'

'Just come and look, Luccy, hmm?' He didn't wait for her to prevaricate further, but took hold of her by the arm, striding out of the kitchen and through to the back of the house before throwing open another door.

If the kitchen was so neat and pristine it looked almost unused, then this room was in chaos! The huge oak desk was overflowing with papers and files and several cups of half-drunk coffee; the bin beside the desk was completely full too, and several drawers had been left open in the filing cabinets along one wall.

Luccy turned to look at Sin as he leant against the wall of the hallway outside, arms crossed over the broadness of his chest as he waited for her reaction. 'This is a mess,' she exclaimed, remembering belatedly that when she had visited him in his hotel suite that evening two months ago it hadn't been particularly tidy, either.

He smiled. 'I'm glad you approve. Wallace is under strict instructions never to enter or touch anything in this room unless he finds himself with a masochistic desire to be parted from a certain part of his anatomy!'

Luccy gave a rueful smile at the unmistakable reference. 'And who is Wallace?'

'Wallace is my—ah, here's the man himself.' He turned as a door opened further down the hallway to admit an elderly gentleman dressed in black trousers and a black waistcoat worn over a snowy white shirt, a grey tie tied meticulously at his throat.

'You have been in the kitchen again, Master Sin,' the elderly man—as English as Luccy was, surprisingly—tutted reprovingly.

A rebuke Sin seemed completely unconcerned by. 'Wallace, come and say hello to Luccy Harper-O'Neill,' he invited warmly.

'Luccy, this is Wallace,' he introduced once the older man had joined them.

'Mr Wallace.' She shook his hand, instinctively liking the kind blue eyes in the elderly man's lined face.

'He insists on just Wallace,' Sin told her ruefully. 'Apparently it isn't the done thing in an English household to call a butler by the title of Mr,' he confided with a gently mocking glance at the older man.

Luccy raised surprised brows. 'You're a butler?'

'I consider myself more in the nature of a nursemaid, Miss Harper-O'Neill,' the elderly man confided dryly. 'Master Sin may be able to run a business empire with aplomb, but without my presence here I doubt that he would even be able to find a clean shirt to put on to go to work in the morning, let alone feed himself.'

'You see what happens when someone has known you since you were two years old—you get absolutely no respect!' Sin said good-humouredly.

Luccy found herself smiling at the obvious affection that existed between the two men.

Sin enjoyed seeing Luccy's obvious bemusement at the addition of Wallace to his household. Maybe persuading her to stay awhile wasn't going to be quite as difficult as he had thought it was going to be…?

He turned to Wallace. 'I was only in your precious kitchen earlier because I was about to make some tea for Miss Harper-O'Neill.'

'Really?' the elderly man said. 'Believe me, Miss Harper-O'Neill, you will be much safer if I make it.

Master Sin has been known to give even boiled water a strange taste!'

'There was something wrong with the water supply that particular day,' Sin protested.

'Of course there was, Master Sin,' the manservant murmured. 'If you would care to take Miss Harper-O'Neill out onto the terrace I will serve tea to you both directly.'

'Luccy?' Sin prompted as he saw she was still rather bemused by Wallace's complete irreverence towards him. But having known the elderly butler for thirty-three of his thirty-five years, Sin considered Wallace as part of his family rather than a servant, and he knew that the affection was returned; the Sinclairs were Wallace's family.

'Sorry.' Luccy grimaced at her own distraction before smiling at the elderly manservant. 'Tea on the terrace would be lovely, thank you,' she accepted.

'Semi-skimmed milk would be healthier than full-fat, Wallace,' Sin put in decisively. 'And perhaps you could add some of your wholesome home-made biscuits, too. Anything else you would like, Luccy?' he asked lightly.

As an afterthought, Luccy felt sure! 'No, you seem to have it pretty well covered,' she answered tartly.

'What did I do this time?' Sin asked once the two of them were outside seated at the green marble table on the terrace, the view incredible, the air warm and clear.

Her eyes flashed as she looked across at him. 'You *are* going to be one of those overprotective prospective fathers!'

He gave an unapologetic shrug. 'I just thought you should eat healthily.'

'I know what I have to do, Sin!'

'Then why are we arguing about it?' he pointed out mildly.

Luccy almost growled in frustration. 'I thought I had already made it plain that I don't like being told what to do.'

'Even when it's in your own best interests?'

'Even then!'

Sin relaxed back in his chair as he looked across at her between narrowed lids. 'I think you're just trying to provoke another argument...'

Maybe she was. But Luccy had seen another side of him since coming to the house, especially since meeting Wallace, and she didn't want to actually start liking Sin. She could even fall in love with him if she allowed herself to do that!

She was only here at all because she was expecting his baby, Luccy reminded herself firmly. Sin only wanted the baby, not her.

And she would do well not to forget that!

'Never mind,' she dismissed. 'I'm sure that Wallace's tea will be wonderful.' It was also obvious that Wallace was the reason the house looked so neat and tidy. 'Have you lived here very long?'

Sin continued to look at her through those narrowed lids, his expression unreadable. 'A couple of years,' he said. 'I got tired of living in the city.'

Luccy nodded. 'It's very peaceful here.' She had often thought she might like to move out of the noise and bustle of London, but as her studio was in London it just hadn't seemed practical.

That might have to change after the baby was born, of course...

'I like it,' Sin said in answer to her comment. 'But I'm quite willing to sell up and move to a different house, either here or in England, if that's what you decide you would like to do.'

She drew in a sharp breath. 'Sin—'

'Luccy?' He quirked dark brows.

This was all going too fast for her!

Way too fast. She was barely used to the fact that she was expecting this man's child, let alone being able to deal with the obvious repercussions of Sin knowing about it too.

'I'm not going to be rushed into making any decisions I might regret, Sin,' she told him firmly.

'Of course not. Obviously we still have at least six months or so before we need to make any definite decision about where we're going to live. But one thing I'm pretty definite on, Luccy…' He sat forward, those grey eyes once again seeming like shimmering mercury. 'I fully intend for you to have my wedding ring safely on your finger before they wheel you into that delivery-room, as you so daintily put it!'

As Luccy looked into those glittering grey eyes she was left in absolutely no doubt that Sin meant every word he said…

CHAPTER EIGHT

'YOU completely took advantage of the fact that you knew I wouldn't argue with you with Wallace present!' Luccy protested indignantly.

Sin arched dark brows as he took in her flushed cheeks and the sparkle in her blue eyes. 'If Wallace hadn't been present I could hardly have asked him to make up the spare bedroom for you, now could I?' he pointed out.

He had waited until they had eaten the tea Wallace had prepared for them—including tempting cakes as well as the delicious home-made biscuits—before mentioning the spare bedroom to the elderly man, wanting to ensure that Luccy had eaten before he introduced any more points of contention into their conversation. As making the practical arrangements for her to stay on here had been guaranteed to do!

She had seemed to relax as they had enjoyed their tea together, by tacit agreement the two of them keeping to non-controversial topics of conversation. Obviously that delicate truce had now come to an end!

'You could at least give me credit for asking Wallace to make up the spare bedroom, rather than simply assuming you would be sharing mine,' Sin pointed out mockingly.

'You can make all the assumptions you like, Sin, but that won't make them fact!' Even that beautiful blue-black hair seemed to crackle with her indignation.

Sin gave a slow, lazy smile. 'You look very beautiful when you're angry.'

'Oh, please!' she groaned disgustedly. 'That line is so hackneyed I can't believe you even said it!'

His smile widened to an appreciative grin. 'Neither can I,' he said, sobering as he looked at her intently. 'But I'm not exaggerating when I tell you that you really are very beautiful,' he added with husky sincerity. 'Even more so now you're pregnant.'

Luccy was very aware of the lurching sensation in her chest at his compliment, a fluttering feeling in her stomach too as she became tinglingly aware of him.

Of the dark thickness of his hair, the intensity of that silver gaze, the sensual curve of his mouth, the powerful width of his chest, and the way the sunlight glittered on the dark hair on his arms as they rested on the table top.

God, she had to get away from this man for a while. Needed some time, and space, in order to get her thoughts together. She felt as if she had been completely railroaded these last few hours.

It certainly didn't help that she was so aware of Sin that she could think of nothing else, be aware of nothing else, that memories of their lovemaking kept intruding into her thoughts, inciting a longing, a yearning, to repeat the experience…

Sin was seducing her just by being there, Luccy realised self-disgustedly. 'Don't you have something else you should be doing other than sitting out here with me?' she asked suddenly.

Sin found Luccy's thoughts easy to read as he saw the self-disgust in her eyes and the return of those lines of strain beside her mouth and eyes. 'I should go back to the office for a couple of hours, yes,' he acknowledged ruefully.

'Then please do so,' she said tautly.

Yes, Luccy most definitely wanted him out of the way for a while. So that she could regather her crumbling defences? Well, he would go along with that for the moment...

He nodded. 'You could just relax here, read a book or take a swim perhaps, and we'll get together again later.'

'At which time it will be too late for me to get any flight back to England today?' she asked.

Sin bit back his impatience. 'Would that really be so bad, Luccy?' he reasoned. 'All I'm asking for at the moment is a little of your time, the chance for us to get to know each other before we decide what to do for the best.'

'Nothing is going to change, Sin.' She sighed. 'No amount of us spending time together is going to alter the fact that you believe I deliberately set out to seduce you two months ago, and for reasons that were far from innocent.'

'*I* was Sin that night.' His mouth had tightened. '*You* seduced Jacob Sinclair the Third.'

'Sin. Jacob Sinclair the Third.' She shrugged. 'They're one and the same person.'

'Actually, they're not,' Sin bit out.

'I see no distinction.'

She didn't *want* to see a distinction, Sin recognised

wryly. Only time would show her that there most definitely was one.

He stood up. 'You'll find plenty of books to read in the sitting-room. The pool and hot tub are at the back of the house—although I'm not sure you should go in the hot tub,' he added with a frown. 'I seem to remember reading on the instructions that pregnant women shouldn't go in.'

Her mouth twisted derisively. 'That's only if you put the jets on.'

'Right. But maybe you should stay out of there, anyway—'

'I think I'm old enough to make my own mind up, Sin!'

He sighed, already knowing from the way Luccy refused to drink any alcohol that she was being conscientious about what she should and shouldn't be doing during her pregnancy. He needed to back off a little.

'Just ring for Wallace if you want anything, hmm?'

'But stay out of his kitchen?' Luccy offered.

'That only applies to me,' Sin retorted. 'I'm sure he won't object in the least if you go in there. I assure you that Wallace is as susceptible as the next man to the charms of a beautiful woman,' he added dryly. 'My mother has him wrapped about her elegant little finger!' He paused beside Luccy's chair to bend down and place a light kiss on her lips.

Luccy was completely unprepared for the caress, her response instinctive as her lips parted beneath his, deepening and lengthening the kiss as one of Sin's hands moved to curve lightly about the nape of her neck.

Sin straightened reluctantly several minutes later to

look down at the flushed confusion on Luccy's face. 'I'll only be a couple of hours,' he promised huskily. 'Just tell Wallace if there's anything you particularly feel like eating for dinner this evening.'

He found himself strangely reluctant to leave. Strangely, because Sin had never allowed a woman, any woman, to interfere with his work before, and yet unbidden thoughts of Luccy these last few months had done so constantly. This reluctance to leave her now was completely out of character, too.

Get a grip, Sinclair, he instantly instructed himself; Luccy had already shown him quite clearly that she didn't feel the same reluctance to be parted from him!

Even so he found himself lingering unnecessarily. 'You'll be okay here on your own?'

Luccy's eyes widened. 'Of course. Besides, I won't be alone, will I?' she added pointedly as Wallace came quietly out onto the terrace to clear away the tea things.

Sin gave the elderly man an affectionate glance. 'I suppose not. Wallace knows where to reach me if you should—'

'Sin, I'm not going to leave without first telling you, if that's what's worrying you.' She arched mocking ebony brows. 'After all, you know where I work, remember?'

Had Sin felt that reluctance to go back into the city because he was worried Luccy might take advantage of his absence to leave?

No, he trusted Luccy enough to at least believe that if she said she would stay here tonight, then she would do it. Besides, he did know where she worked!

His hesitation was for quite another reason, he recognised with an inward frown. In spite of everything he was still totally physically aware of Luccy. At the same time, he felt protective because she was carrying his child. Even if it was a protectiveness that Luccy obviously resented.

'Sin, will you just go to work?' Luccy said with a little laugh as he remained beside her. 'I really don't need a nursemaid.'

'I'm well aware of the fact that you're a grown woman.'

'Then try treating me like one!'

He looked down at her silently for several more seconds before giving an abrupt nod of his head. 'I should be back in plenty of time for dinner,' he rasped harshly before turning sharply on his heel and walking back inside the house.

Luccy stared after him. What on earth had all that been about?

Maybe Sin was just feeling the strain of them being together here? After all, he was no more used to sharing his home with anyone—the devoted Wallace apart—than she was.

Well, Sin needn't worry too much about that; Luccy had no intention of staying on here any longer than she absolutely had to in order to convince Sin that she was quite capable of taking care of herself—and anyone else who came along!

'What the—? Sin, you scared the hell out of me!' The water swirled wildly about Luccy as she surged up in the hot tub—minus the jets—to turn and glare at him, at the same time dislodging his hands from where they had been cupping her breasts beneath the water.

Sin looked down at her unrepentantly, his shirt sleeves dripping with water from being submerged in the hot tub.

He had returned to the house only a few minutes

ago and learnt from Wallace that Luccy was outside on the deck relaxing in the hot tub, sparing only a few seconds to discard the jacket to his suit before going outside to join her.

Sin had watched her unobserved for several minutes. Luccy was obviously completely relaxed as she lay back in the warm water with her eyes closed, the slight smile that curved her lips telling him that her thoughts were at least pleasant ones.

It would be too much to hope that those thoughts might be of the two of them making love, of course, but Sin found himself unable to think of anything else but making love to Luccy as she sat there looking so temptingly beautiful; her face was glowingly lovely in the early evening sunlight, that long ebony-blue hair loosely secured on top of her head, completely exposing the long, creamy expanse of her neck and throat. The tee shirt she wore was clinging wetly to the firm thrust of her breasts just beneath the water, the darker nipples clearly visible against the white material.

Sin had moved stealthily to the side of the tub before bending down behind Luccy, his hands instinctively curving about the thrust of those breasts even as he bent to taste the creamy expanse of her throat with his lips.

A familiarity Luccy had obviously taken exception to!

'You might at least have given me some sort of warning that you were there!' Luccy could feel the embarrassed colour heating her cheeks even as she continued to glare up at Sin, aware that her breasts were totally aroused from the unexpectedness of Sin's hands cupping them in that way.

'Coughed, you mean?' he taunted even as he began to unbutton his wet shirt.

'Something like— What are you doing?' she demanded sharply as Sin finished unbuttoning his shirt before taking it off completely and dropping it down onto the wooden decking.

'I thought I might join you,' he told her huskily as he slipped off his shoes and socks before unfastening his trousers.

'I—but—you can't, Sin!' Luccy shook her head frantically as he removed his trousers and stood there wearing only figure-hugging black boxers that left absolutely nothing to the imagination—as they proudly showed off the firm thrust of his arousal!

He paused with his thumbs hooked into the waistband of those boxers. 'Why can't I?'

Any number of reasons that Luccy could think of. All of them to do with the fact that she simply wasn't used to having a man strip naked in front of her. Even—no, especially—a man she knew as intimately as she knew Sin. And who knew her just as intimately.

Luccy swallowed hard. 'Look, I'll get out and—'

'If it makes you feel more comfortable, I'll keep my boxers on,' Sin offered as he unhooked his thumbs to look down at her mockingly.

'Keeping your boxers on isn't going to make the slightest difference— That was not an invitation for you to remove them!' Luccy gasped as Sin did exactly that, instantly rendering her speechless.

Oh, God…

Sin was beautiful. Absolutely, completely, totally male and utterly beautiful.

The darkness of his hair grew slightly overlong to rest on the broad expanse of his shoulders, his face like a bronzed mask in the evening sunlight, chest muscled, stomach flat, his thighs—oh, dear Lord, those thighs!—firm and muscled as they flanked his blatant arousal, his legs long and lightly dusted with dark hair. Even Sin's feet were beautifully shaped.

In the course of her work Luccy had worked with lots of male models over the years, in all states of dress and undress, but none of them had been as ruggedly compelling as Sin. Or made her senses sing in awareness…

'Can I get in now or do you want to look some more?'

Luccy's embarrassed gaze returned to Sin's mockingly handsome face. 'I really wasn't in a—position, to look before,' she came back tartly to cover that embarrassment.

'Feel free,' Sin invited huskily, grey eyes gleaming like silver.

Luccy instantly turned away from all that blatant maleness. 'Don't be ridiculous, Sin,' she snapped dismissively, deliberately keeping her gaze averted when she felt the water move slightly as Sin climbed into the hot-tub with her, the long length of Sin's thigh brushing against hers as he sat down beside her. 'It's probably time I was getting out anyway—'

'Stay, Luccy,' he encouraged throatily, so close now that the warmth of his breath disturbed the loose tendrils of hair beside her exposed ear, his arm curved along the top of the wooden tub behind her. 'Did you miss me?' he asked softly.

Luccy was totally unnerved by Sin's close proximity, her shoulders tensed as she sat slightly away from the back of the tub in order to avoid coming into contact with the warmth of his arm. 'You've only been gone a couple of hours,' she pointed out.

Strangely, though, she *had* missed him, the house

having suddenly felt very empty with only herself and Wallace in residence. But Luccy didn't intend telling Sin that!

'So I have,' he murmured ruefully, his arm bending slightly behind her as his fingers began to play with the loose tendrils of hair at her nape. 'Did you think of me while I was away?' he added gruffly.

'No, of course not—' Luccy had turned sharply to look at him, and then wished she hadn't as she found her face now only inches away from his, those silver-grey eyes totally mesmerising.

Sin had certainly found himself thinking of Luccy while he'd been in the city the past couple of hours!

None of his previous relationships had ever involved actually living with a woman, and with the penthouse suite at the Sinclair Hotel at his disposal he'd never brought women back to his home in order to sleep with them, either.

The clinging wet tee shirt Luccy was wearing revealed more than it concealed as Sin felt his gaze once again drawn to the darkness of her nipples so clearly outlined against the white material, and he wondered what else she was wearing...

Another of those scraps of lace, he discovered as his hand moved caressingly along the length of her thigh to her hip. Black this time, he found as he moved her tee shirt slightly to one side so that he could touch the warmth of her waist before cupping the fullness of her breast, watching the way Luccy's eyes darkened, her lips slightly parted as the soft pad of his thumb moved across the rigid nipple.

'You're thinking of me now, though, hmm?' he murmured.

'Of how you like my hands touching you. Of how it would feel if I were to bend down and suck—'

'Don't, Sin,' she groaned breathlessly.

'Why not?' he challenged huskily as he looked up and saw the flush of arousal on her cheeks.

'Because I won't become another of the women you seduce in your hot tub!' she roused herself enough to protest.

'Another of the women I seduce in my hot tub?' he repeated incredulously.

'No,' Luccy insisted tautly as she very firmly removed Sin's wandering hand before moving slightly away from him.

'What makes you think I have a parade of women through here?' Sin asked curiously.

'The costume I found in the changing-room,' Luccy snapped. 'The costume with a 36C top.'

'And you are?'

'At the moment? A 32D, and growing,' she added ruefully; Luccy had always been slightly disappointed that her bust size had stopped when she reached the age of sixteen, but she had definitely started to expand in that area since becoming pregnant.

Sin's gaze warmed appreciatively. 'I'm not complaining.'

'Sin—'

'The costume in the changing-room belongs to my mother, Luccy,' he interrupted.

She blinked. 'Your mother?'

Sin was so close to Luccy now that he could see the darker flecks of blue in her eyes. Those beautiful blue eyes that a man could lose his soul in...

'My mother uses that costume when she's here,' he

expanded, wondering suddenly whether *he* was in danger of losing his soul to her. 'I never bring women here, Luccy,' he assured her even as he gave in to the temptation to allow his lips to once more taste the creamy expanse of her throat.

That throat moved convulsively as Luccy swallowed. 'You brought *me* here.'

'Ah, but you aren't "women",' Sin murmured as he tasted the lobe of her ear now.

'I'm not?'

'Not at all,' Sin responded. 'You're the future mother of my children, and the future mistress of this house.'

Until that moment, the owner of that black bathing costume now explained, Luccy had been in danger of succumbing to the air of intimacy that surrounded them, of losing herself totally in Sin's seduction. But this stark reminder of Sin's intention of seducing her into marrying him completely evaporated her rapidly escalating arousal.

She moved sharply away from him. 'I said don't, Sin!' she repeated more firmly as she stood up and moved towards the step to get out, totally uncaring of the way the white tee shirt clung to her; after all, there was nothing there that Sin hadn't already seen, touched, or kissed!

'Why the hell not?' he growled as he looked across at her.

'I am not going to be the mother of your children or the future mistress of this house!' Luccy was breathing hard in her agitation.

'That's exactly what you're going to be—'

'No, it is *not*!' Luccy turned back to face him, her face flushed with anger now. 'I allowed you to bring me here only so that we could discuss future arrangements for after the baby is born. I've already told you why I have absolutely no intention of marrying you, let alone having other children with you.'

Sin's mouth was a taut line. 'And I've already told you that the alternative, my setting you up in a house somewhere and then only being allowed agreed visitation rights, is not an option, either!'

'I haven't asked for any of that—'

'What other alternatives are there?' he rasped coldly. 'Come on, Luccy, if neither of those is acceptable, what else is there?'

'I don't know.' Tears glistened in her eyes. 'I just know that I can't marry a man—any man—because I'm expecting his baby!'

Sin nodded grimly. 'Because your sister did and the marriage was a disaster.'

'Well, it was!' Luccy cried. 'She and Rory despise each other now.'

'And you think that might happen to us, too?'

'You don't particularly like me now, so, yes, in eight years' time you'll probably hate the sight of me.'

'Oh, I like you now, Luccy,' he muttered.

Luccy shot him an impatient glare. 'You're talking about in a sexual way!'

He shrugged bare shoulders. 'It's a good place to start.'

'It's a good place to finish, too!'

Sin's expression was grim. 'We have at least one advantage over your sister and her ex-husband that I can see.'

Luccy tensed warily. 'Which is?'

His mouth twisted derisively. 'You would be marrying a billionaire—'

'Sin, don't you *dare* start accusing me again of wanting you for your money,' she warned angrily. 'I've seen how most rich men treat their wives, and I can assure you that I have no intention of marrying you and being left in this house like some—some—'

'Some *what*?' Sin asked, dangerously soft.

'Some trophy on the mantel—' Luccy made it sound like an insult '—while no doubt you remain in the city night after night, at your conveniently "always available" suite at the Sinclair Hotel, entertaining your girlfriends!'

Sin's mouth tightened at how close a description it was to the way his life was now. But that was as a single man. It would be different when Luccy was his wife. 'You're asking for fidelity, is that it?'

'No, that is not it!' Luccy said heatedly. 'Don't you see, Sin? I just don't want to marry you!'

Yes, Sin did see—it was just that there was no other alternative that was acceptable to him.

'I'm expecting your baby, so therefore I must become your wife.' Luccy shook her head in utter denial. Then she said, coolly and calmly, 'No way, Sin. Absolutely no way will I ever marry a man for that reason.'

Sin could only watch in absolute frustration as Luccy climbed out of the hot tub before pulling on her robe and marching back into the house, her cheeks flushed with temper, her head proudly high, and her shoulders stiff with resolve.

It was a resolve Sin had every intention of breaking.

One way or another…

CHAPTER NINE

'YOU'RE looking very beautiful this evening.'

Luccy eyed Sin warily, having joined him outside on the terrace for a drink before dinner—wine for Sin, once again a glass of sparkling water for Luccy—and finding herself once again slightly unnerved by the pleasantness of his tone as he commented on the midnight-blue knee-length dress she wore, her hair loose and gleaming about her shoulders.

Quite what she had expected Sin's mood to be after their disagreement earlier, she didn't know, but she certainly hadn't expected his first words to be a compliment on her appearance!

'Thank you,' she accepted huskily, having no intention of telling Sin how devastatingly handsome he looked in the black evening suit and snowy white shirt he had changed into. If she didn't mention it perhaps she could ignore it. Maybe. Although she somehow doubted it. Distance, that was what she needed. If not physically, then at least verbally.

'Sin, we still haven't resolved our differences of opinion concerning the future—'

'Not now, Luccy,' Sin cut in firmly. 'Let's just

enjoy the peace and beauty of the evening, instead, hmm?'

Enjoying the peace and beauty of the evening wasn't a good idea when Luccy was so aware of Sin that just being alone with him like this was making her toes curl!

That air of intimacy, the total physical awareness, was so thick and heavy between them now that Luccy almost felt as if she could reach out and touch it. As she wanted to reach out and touch Sin...

Luccy could barely breathe, let alone make the conversation she knew was necessary to dispel that air of expectation, as if they were both poised on the brink of—

The brink of what?

Luccy stiffened her spine, determined to dispel this air of intimacy between them once and for all. 'Sin, I've decided that it really would be for the best if I went back to England tomorrow.'

Sin had been determined, after their disagreement earlier, to make this a pleasant evening for both of them, with no discord between them, and now Luccy had introduced—deliberately?—the one subject sure to cause a resumption of that contention.

'I would much rather continue telling you how beautiful you are,' he said instead.

She gave him a reproving look. 'To what purpose?'

He frowned. 'Sorry?'

Luccy sighed. 'Sin, I've fallen for your seduction routine once already—'

'Don't you have that rather confused?' he rasped, suddenly appearing very intimidating in the rapidly darkening evening.

She met his gaze unblinkingly. 'That's not the way I remember it.'

Sin narrowed his eyes to steely slits. 'As I recall you were as out of control that night as I was.'

Her mouth tightened, her cheeks flushed. 'I think it's extremely ungentlemanly of you to keep reminding me of that.'

Yes, it was, Sin acknowledged frustratedly. Very much so. His Southern Mama would be appalled. It was just that Luccy's constant dismissal of their physical response to each other was beginning to annoy the hell out of him.

He drew in a deeply controlling breath as he opted for a less controversial subject. 'What did you ask Wallace to prepare for our dinner this evening?'

Luccy accepted the subject change and gave a rueful grimace. 'I didn't. Wallace seemed to welcome the opportunity of my being here to prepare the full English roast beef and vegetables,' she explained with a shake of her head. 'I didn't like to disappoint him.'

'It's a pity you don't feel the same consideration where I'm concerned,' Sin drawled derisively.

'Sin—'

'Okay, okay, I'm sorry.' He held up his hands in apology. 'I shouldn't have said that.'

'No, you shouldn't,' Luccy agreed. She closed her eyes briefly, then took a deep breath. 'Sin, I'm really not sure I can do this.'

'It's only dinner, Luccy.'

'I wasn't talking about dinner, and you know it!' She glared her exasperation with his deliberate misunderstanding. 'Our being here together like this, I— Can't you see how destructive it is? We can't have a single conversation without it either resulting in an argument or one of us insulting the other.'

'Maybe if we chose an innocuous subject like the weather…' he teased.

Luccy sighed. 'We would probably even disagree about that.'

Sin eyed her searchingly, knowing by the pallor of Luccy's cheeks that she really was finding all of this a strain. 'Why do you suppose that is?'

'I don't know,' she said.

'Don't you?'

She eyed him warily, her throat moving convulsively as she swallowed. 'Do you?'

Sin smiled. 'Oh, yes, I know.'

Her expression became even more wary. 'And…?'

Sin's answer was to reach out and touch one of her creamy cheeks, his mouth tightening slightly as she flinched before relaxing against that caress. 'We want each other, Luccy. It's as simple—or as complicated—as that,' he murmured huskily, knowing it was the truth.

He wanted Luccy. Wanted to make love with her. And no matter how much she tried to deny it, he knew that she wanted him too.

It was there between them, deep and heavy, almost touchable, every time they were anywhere near each other.

Luccy moistened suddenly dry lips, unable to look away from the compelling glitter of Sin's eyes. 'Then it's complicated.'

'Why is it?'

'Because—' She drew in a ragged breath. 'Because it is. Can't you see?'

'Luccy, the only thing I can see or feel at the moment is you.' Sin stepped closer to her, his breath a warm caress against her temple. 'Let's uncomplicate it, Luccy,' he murmured.

Her gaze, along with everything else, was captivated. 'How?'

'By at least enjoying what we have, of course.'

'Sex!' Luccy exclaimed.

Sin's face had darkened. 'If that's what you choose to call it, yes.'

'What else could it be called?' she asked wearily as she stepped away from him. 'Wallace will be waiting for us to go in to dinner—'

'I'm sure Wallace knows when not to interrupt,' Sin grated, a nerve pulsing in one tightly clenched cheek. 'Luccy, the tension between us—the sexual tension, if that's what you insist on calling it,' he amended harshly at her disparaging look. 'It's creating an impossible situation between us.'

'So your answer is for us to go to bed together, is that it?' Her head was back challengingly as she met his glittering silver gaze full on.

'Look on the bright side—at least we know you can't get pregnant!'

Luccy gave a pained gasp as she moved jerkily away from him. 'That was truly unforgivable!' She shook her head. 'I— Could you please make my apologies to Wallace? I really don't think I could eat any dinner.'

'Maybe you would prefer it if I made my excuses instead?'

'I still wouldn't be able to eat anything,' she choked. 'I—excuse me!' She turned and almost ran back inside the house.

Sin stared after her in concern. Damn it, he didn't want to argue with her. Or make her cry…

* * *

Several hours later Sin stood outside on the darkened terrace, staring sightlessly across the acres of meadow and woodland now bathed in moonlight, regretting for the first time in many years that he had given up smoking even the occasional cigar—he could have certainly done with one right now!

Dinner had been an endless affair, with Sin almost able to feel Wallace's disapproval of the fact that Luccy wasn't present, as if the older man was well aware that Sin was responsible for her absence. Which he definitely was, Sin acknowledged ruefully; Wallace had an uncanny sixth sense that seemed to inform him of everything that transpired in the house he ran with such quiet efficiency.

It was well after midnight now, and Luccy had probably been asleep for hours, but Sin felt too restless to retire to his own bedroom, knowing that he wouldn't be able to sleep even if he did.

How could he possibly go to sleep when he knew Luccy was in another bedroom only a short distance away?

How could he forget the tears he had seen in her eyes earlier as she had run away from him?

'Master Sin?'

He drew in a deep, weary breath before turning to face Wallace. 'Yes?'

The elderly man's expression was slightly less stiff and disapproving than it had been earlier this evening. 'I thought you might be interested to know that Miss Harper-O'Neill came to the kitchen for a hot drink a few minutes ago.'

Not asleep yet, after all?

Sin looked at the older man searchingly. Wallace

knew better than anyone that Sin did not bring women here. Just as he must be wondering why Sin had made Luccy the exception 'She did?' he finally murmured.

Wallace nodded. 'She looked as if she may have been…crying.' A slight censure could once again be heard in his tone.

Deservedly so, Sin thought. 'Tell me, Wallace,' he mused heavily, 'what would you do if you knew you had behaved like a complete bastard to the woman who—' He broke off, frowning, sure that Luccy wouldn't appreciate him telling Wallace—or anyone else yet—about her pregnancy. Sin wasn't too happy himself with anyone else knowing, either, until the two of them had resolved the situation to his own satisfaction.

Wallace answered him anyway. 'I think you already know, Master Sin, that an apology is in order. That it is not polite to behave like any sort of bastard to a female guest in your home, let alone someone as lovely as Miss Harper-O'Neill.'

It shouldn't have surprised Sin that Luccy had managed to succeed in charming Wallace; she seemed to charm every male she met, of whatever age. Even his grandfather had—

God, he was even *thinking* like a bastard now!

'Even if…' Sin paused, choosing his words carefully. 'Even if a part of you—a large part of you—still believed you had done nothing wrong?'

'It is especially important that the man apologise in those circumstances, Master Sin.'

Sin eyed the older man. 'When did you get to be so knowledgeable about women, Wallace?' Wallace had been with the family for over thirty years now, and as far as Sin was aware there had never been a woman in his life during those years.

'I believe it may have been from observing your father's behaviour towards your mother...'

'Oh.'

Amusement gleamed in the older man's eyes. 'Yes, Master Sin.'

Sin knew that his father had always found it more politically correct—and less of a strain!—to be the one to bring an end to an argument with the beautiful and fiery Claudia.

He gave the elderly butler a small smile. 'Thank you, Wallace. I believe you are quite correct. As usual.'

'Thank you, Master Sin.' Wallace nodded. 'If there is nothing else I can get you this evening...?'

He grimaced. 'A gun might be useful!'

'If you think that would solve the problem, Master Sin,' the butler said calmly. 'Personally, I've always found that an apology—a sincere apology—usually does the trick.'

Sin grinned. 'And if it doesn't?'

Wallace shrugged. 'Then at least one has the personal satisfaction of knowing that one tried. If you're sure that is all, I will wish you goodnight, Master Sin.'

''Night, Wallace,' Sin returned distractedly.

Would Luccy even listen to any apology that Sin made? Probably not. But, as Wallace had so succinctly pointed out, at least he would have tried...

'Yes...?' Luccy warily answered the soft knock that had sounded on her bedroom door seconds ago, expecting to find Wallace standing outside, her eyes widening in alarm as she found herself looking at Sin instead as he stood so tall and imposing in the hallway.

She had switched on the light on the table beside her bed before getting out of bed, pulling a matching robe on over her peach silk nightgown. She clutched that robe about her now as she faced Sin defensively. 'Yes?'

He looked at her quizzically. 'Wallace seemed to think you were having trouble sleeping…'

So she had Wallace to thank for Sin's presence outside her bedroom!

Much as she had taken a liking to the elderly butler, Luccy couldn't help wishing that on this occasion he had been less than his efficient self.

'He insisted on making me a hot chocolate, so I'm sure I shall be able to sleep now,' she dismissed.

Sin nodded, his gaze guarded now. 'I believe I owe you an apology.'

Luccy stiffened. She had spent a most miserable evening sitting in her bedroom, alternating between feeling angry and then tearful as she'd brooded over Sin's earlier remarks to her. She knew he still believed that she had made a deliberate play for him the night they'd met, and there didn't seem any way Luccy could convince him otherwise, but did he have to be so nasty about it? Yes, she was pregnant, but if he thought she was any happier about the hand fate had dealt her—and he obviously did—then he was mistaken; she had just decided that she couldn't change what already was.

She looked at him coldly. 'Really?'

That coldness was completely wasted on Sin as all he could see was the way the lamplight reflected behind Luccy, rendering her robe and nightgown almost see-through to show him tantalising glimpses of firm uptilting breasts, her slender waist, and the delicious curve of her hips.

Her hair was loose and silky about her shoulders and cascading, blue-black, down the length of her spine, her face completely bare of make-up.

To Sin she had never looked more beautiful...

'Well?' she prompted uncertainly at his continued silence.

Sin brought himself back to an awareness of why he was actually here. It certainly wasn't to ogle Luccy in her nightgown! 'I shouldn't have made that remark earlier about getting pregnant.'

'No, you shouldn't.'

Sin gave a rueful smile. 'You don't intend making this easy for me, do you?'

She arched one dark brow. 'Should I?'

'No,' he acknowledged with a sigh. 'What I said was unforgivable. I apologise.'

Luccy felt a slight softening of her anger at the stiffly made apology. She very much doubted that the arrogant Jacob Sinclair the Third felt the need to make too many of them—which was probably why he sounded so out of practice!

She gave an inclination of her head. 'Your apology is accepted.'

'Good.' Sin nodded his satisfaction. 'So we'll begin tomorrow as if tonight never happened?'

She raised dark brows. 'I wouldn't go that far...'

'For God's sake, Luccy—' Sin broke off, drawing in a deep, controlling breath. 'You're right. I'll leave it. We'll talk about this again tomorrow.' He had to get out of here! Now! Before those tantalising glimpses of her curvaceous body drove him insane!

Luccy frowned slightly. 'Sin?'

'Yes?' he grated between clenched teeth, a nerve pulsing in his tensed cheek.

'What's wrong now?' She sighed. 'What could I possibly have done wrong in the past few seconds—?'

'You haven't done anything wrong, damn it!' Sin rasped as he found himself unable to look away from her, the naked hunger visible in his eyes.

A blush slowly crept up her cheeks. 'Oh…'

'Yes—oh,' Sin muttered. 'Perhaps this wasn't such a good idea. I should have waited until the morning.'

'Sin?'

'Don't look at me like that, Luccy!' Every part of him was tense and aching. For Luccy. For the feel of her naked against him.

Her tongue moved nervously across her lips. 'How am I looking at you?'

'With the same hunger I'm feeling for you,' Sin groaned achingly. 'Luccy, I don't want sex from you, I want to make love with you. I want to kiss and caress every delectable inch of you. From your head to your toes. Will you allow me to do that?'

Would she? Luccy wondered shakily.

Hadn't she felt that same aching desire the moment she had opened her bedroom door and seen him standing there?

Yes, of course she had…

It wouldn't solve anything. It wouldn't change anything. But she wanted it, anyway!

'Come in,' she invited huskily as she stood back to open the door wider so that Sin could enter her bedroom.

His gaze didn't leave hers as he stepped inside and

closed the door behind him. Luccy moved willingly into his arms as they curved about her waist and the heat of his lips travelled the length of her throat, his tongue a soft rasp against her skin.

She gave a gasp as Sin's teeth nibbled her ear lobe, her throat arching and her hands clinging to the broadness of his shoulders as desire jolted through her body almost like an electric shock.

Sin wanted Luccy so strongly, so powerfully, that he had to fight to maintain control as the hard throb of his body cried out for possession of hers.

She tasted wonderful, so soft and creamy, the perfume of her hair surrounding him, both of them, as his lips sought and found hers.

'From your head to your toes, Luccy,' he promised gruffly as he swung her up into his arms and carried her over to the bed, laying her down on the cool sheet before taking off his jacket and dropping it on the floor before joining her there.

She looked so beautiful as she lay looking up at him. So damned beautiful!

He kissed her eyes first, then her nose, then those luscious lips once more, lingering there before moving on to her chin, her creamy neck, the dark hollows at the base of her throat, pushing her robe aside to bare the tops of her breasts to his questing lips and tongue.

'Sit up for me,' he groaned huskily, slipping the robe down her arms as she did so before sliding the strap of her gown down too and baring one of her breasts.

It was fuller than he remembered, the nipple darker, bigger, already hard and roused as he lowered his head and his tongue moved slowly, lightly, erotically over that hardened tip, knowing he was giving Luccy pleasure as she arched into him, her hands moving to cradle his head.

Sin teased that aching nipple mercilessly, kissing, licking, laving, biting gently, before drawing it greedily into the hot cavern of his mouth, his hand cupping its twin and moving the soft pad of his thumb on her nipple in the same rhythmic caress.

Luccy's body felt as if it were on fire, every part of her alive and vibrating with the desire Sin ignited inside her, his lips against her breasts only assuaging part of that need as the ache between her thighs rose unbearably.

She needed to touch him too, to feel his naked flesh against hers. Her fingers were clumsy in their haste to undo the buttons on his shirt so that she could bare his shoulders and chest, to kiss and taste him, teeth gently biting as her hair cascaded over them like silk.

'Your head to your toes, Luccy,' Sin reminded her again as he moved back slightly to take his shirt off completely before lifting her nightgown over her head to bare her completely to his hungry gaze.

Her breasts really were fuller, sloping gently above her narrow waist, her hips and thighs a tempting curve, dark curls nestling at their apex.

He began at her breasts, placing gentle kisses against those tempting tips before moving lower, to the gentle slope beneath, and then down to her waist, the caress even gentler as he placed a kiss where his child nestled inside her, his hands following that same path.

Luccy lay back on the pillows, her eyes closing as she felt Sin's hands like butterfly wings against her thighs, parting her, running his fingers lightly, arousingly against her wetness before finding the nub that nestled amongst her ebony curls. He began to caress her there, slowly, pleasurably, on and on, until Luccy thought she might faint with the pleasure of it.

She cried out at the first touch of Sin's lips against her, shocked, and then totally lost as his tongue moved in an erotic caress. She gasped as she felt the climax building inside her, Sin's hands moving down to grasp her hips to hold her against him, his tongue driving her completely over the edge as she felt the pleasure engulf and claim her.

It was beyond anything Luccy had ever experienced before. Beyond even what the two of them had shared before, and she hadn't believed there would ever be anything better than that.

She wanted more!

Needed more.

Wanted to give Sin more.

He offered no resistance as she moved up to press him down onto the pillows, her gaze holding his as she unfastened his trousers, the descent of the zip slightly hindered by the firmness of his arousal, that pulsing shaft leaping free seconds later as Luccy removed the last of his clothes.

He was beautiful. Hard. Muscled. Lean.

The darkness of his hair was tousled about his shoulders from her wildly caressing fingers, his chest and stomach all muscled ridges, his arousal jutting out long and hard, and pulsing beneath her fingers as she reached out to curl them about that arousal, her other hand moving lower to cup and hold him.

Sin groaned hoarsely as he felt Luccy's lips and tongue against him, tasting the length of him, before she moved to take him into the moist heat of her mouth.

He was too aroused already, needed to be inside her too much to be able to take those caresses for long, reaching down to move her up and over him, leaving Sin's own hands free to cup and caress her breasts.

Luccy's back arched as she set the rhythm above him, her hips moving slowly, erotically as she rode Sin, feeling the tension building inside him. He moved so that he could take her breast into his mouth as Luccy rode him harder and faster.

Luccy could feel a second climax building inside her even as she heard Sin's groan, his release sending those shock waves crashing wildly into a climax that threatened to shatter her, and him, into a million pieces.

Minutes—hours?—later, Luccy collapsed weakly onto Sin's chest, her breathing ragged as she trembled with the force of that second, mind-shattering release.

She should regret this. She knew that she should. But she didn't. How could she possibly regret something that had been so wonderful? So much a joining, with an equality of giving and taking that had rendered their lovemaking totally beautiful.

And it had been love, Luccy realised dazedly.

On her part, at least.

Dear God, she was in love with Sin!

She was in love with a man who didn't trust her, let alone love her in return!

Was that why his earlier remarks had hurt so much? Why she hadn't been able to resist him when he had come to her bedroom?

How could she possibly have been so stupid?

Sin had never known such aching arousal followed by such an earth-shattering release. He felt completely spent, and totally satiated even as he felt Luccy's withdrawal, not just emotionally but physically too as she moved to lie on the bed beside him, long lashes lowered over those midnight-blue eyes.

What was she thinking? he wondered with a gathering frown.

Nothing pleasant, if he was reading this situation correctly!

Did she regret what had just happened?

She couldn't regret it!

No matter what other plans Luccy might have for her own life, and consequently that of their child, didn't she realise that what they had just shared was unusual, a compatibility that all couples sought and so rarely ever found?

'Luccy—'

'It's been a very—strange day, and now I think I would like to get some sleep, if you don't mind, Sin,' she said flatly, her gaze still not quite meeting his.

Sin turned on his side to look down at her, not touching her, not daring to touch her. 'Luccy, do you regret what just happened?'

Her lids flew wide. 'Of course I—! Yes, I regret it,' she said more calmly. 'As I said earlier, it changes nothing. I'm still not going to marry you.'

Changes nothing!

Damn it, couldn't Luccy see that what they had just shared gave them a basis on which to build a marriage? That maybe, in time, she might even come to love him? That he might come to love her, too? Damn it, he desired her so much he was probably halfway there already. With a little cooperation from Luccy—

'I think you have made your point, Sin, and now I would like you to leave,' Luccy told him coldly; she wouldn't just *like* him to leave, she *needed* him to leave! She was going to break down and start crying again in a minute, and she really didn't want Sin to be a witness to that.

'I made my point?' he repeated softly, icily. 'And exactly what point would that be?' His voice hardened noticeably.

Luccy's mouth firmed. 'That great sex can make us forget all sorts of things,' she said. 'It even made us forget for a while that we don't even like each other.'

Sin felt as if Luccy had physically punched him in the stomach. She still claimed she didn't even like him?

He sat up abruptly. 'Then I guess we'll just have to settle for great sex, won't we?' he grated.

'What do you mean?' She looked up at him warily as he began to pull his clothes back on.

'I mean, Luccy, that once we're married—because we *are* getting married,' he assured her firmly. 'I'm going to share your bed—our bed—every night. And every damned day too if I feel like it!' He didn't bother with the buttons on his shirt as he bent down to pick up his jacket from the carpet.

Her cheeks flushed with her own rising temper. 'You can't force me into marrying you—'

'Oh, yes, Luccy, I really believe that I can.'

Luccy's breath caught in her throat as she heard the steel in Sin's voice. 'Because of the baby?'

'Why else?' Sin gave a humourless smile.

She shook her head. 'You would condemn our child to being brought up in a loveless marriage?'

His jaw was tight. 'You know the alternative, Luccy.'

She wrapped her arms protectively about her body. 'I'm not going to give you my baby!'

'*My* baby, Luccy,' he corrected. 'The legitimate Sinclair heir. And I'll fight you for it in court if I have to.'

Luccy's eyes glittered with a mixture of anger and tears. 'If you force me into this, Sin, then I will hate you for the rest of my life!'

'Hate away, Luccy,' he said. 'There's an old adage that my grandfather taught me long ago—keep your friends close, but your enemies even closer. Well, I intend keeping you very close for the next fifty years or so.'

'I am *not* your enemy—'

'That's the real problem, isn't it, Luccy? I still have no idea what you are. One minute I'm convinced that you're a conniving little witch, and the next you seem like something totally different.'

Luccy shook her head sadly. 'Because you're too blinded by your own prejudice to see the truth. Another woman used you, years ago, and because a lying adulterous creep like Paul Bridger told you I had done the same thing, you chose to believe him! Can't you see, you'll never understand me while you continue to believe that?'

Sin's mouth was a thin, taut line as he looked down at her coldly for several long seconds before turning on his heel and leaving the bedroom, the door closing with soft violence behind him.

Luccy stared after him, dazed and disorientated by the anger that had followed their exquisite lovemaking.

Completely devastated by the knowledge that, in spite of everything, she was deeply in love with him…

CHAPTER TEN

SIN stood up from the breakfast table as Luccy walked out onto the terrace wearing a red tee shirt and flowing white linen skirt, his expression remote. The fact that he was wearing a tailored grey suit, snowy white shirt, and a silver tie knotted meticulously at his throat told her that he was probably going into the city today.

Just as if nothing had happened between them last night.

Not their lovemaking, at least. Because the anger was most definitely still there as he silently moved to hold a chair back for Luccy to sit down at the table before resuming his own seat opposite.

It wasn't a pleasant silence. Nor a comfortable one. But with Wallace present Luccy knew that she couldn't resume their conversation of last night, either.

And she wanted to.

She hadn't slept at all well after Sin had left her, reliving his last words over and over inside her head. He was as determined to marry her as she was not to marry him!

'Coffee, Miss Harper-O'Neill?'

She turned to smile at Wallace as he hovered beside

the table holding a coffee pot. 'I would prefer tea if it isn't too much trouble?'

'Not at all,' the elderly butler assured her warmly. 'Can I get you anything to eat? Eggs? Bacon? Or perhaps some sweet Scottish kippers?' he added temptingly.

Except Luccy wasn't tempted, just the mention of fish—any fish—enough to make her stomach churn in protest.

She had been lucky in her pregnancy so far in that she hadn't experienced morning sickness, but just the mention of fish, let alone the smell of it, was enough to make her feel ill.

'Forget the kippers, Wallace,' Sin instructed after a glance at Luccy's rapidly paling face, recalling only too well how ill she had been the last time she had been presented with a plate of fish. 'Perhaps just some tea and fresh toast for the moment, Wallace,' he suggested ruefully.

'Thank you,' Luccy murmured softly once they were alone on the terrace, her gaze not quite meeting his.

'You're welcome,' Sin drawled dryly. 'Luccy, I'm not going to disappear just because you don't look at me!' he added impatiently as she continued to stare out at the parkland.

Her eyes glittered as she turned sharply back to him. 'Pity!'

'Isn't it?' Sin's mouth twisted self-derisively. 'I'm sure you'll be pleased to know that I have to go in to the office today.'

She nodded. 'I think that would be best.'

Sin bit back his biting retort, knowing that this constant tension between them couldn't be good for either her or the baby.

But it wasn't helping his effort at detachment that

Luccy was looking so ethereally beautiful this morning. Her long hair was braided down her spine, her eyes huge blue pools in the otherwise paleness of her face, her cheeks slightly hollow, her exposed throat looking delicate, her body still amazingly slender in the red tee shirt and white linen skirt.

She needed to eat more. It was because they had argued—yet again!—that she had missed dinner the previous evening...

His mouth tightened. 'Perhaps with me gone you might actually manage to eat something this morning?'

'Perhaps I will.'

Sin sighed. 'Luccy, is this what it's going to be like when we're married?'

She gave him a sweetly insincere smile. 'Not very pleasant, is it?'

Hellish more aptly described it!

But he was trying—he really was!—not to have another argument with her this morning.

Luccy didn't look as if she had got much sleep after they had parted last night, but neither had Sin as he had tossed and turned restlessly in his bed, the memory of their last bitter argument refusing to go away. Sin had resolved that he would not argue with Luccy again this morning.

He wasn't doing too well so far.

'I'll go then.' He stood up abruptly.

She looked away. 'Goodbye.'

'Luccy—'

'Sin.' She turned back and met his gaze challengingly.

Sin fought an inner battle with his frustrated anger. 'This isn't helping at all, you know,' he finally bit out tautly.

She arched dark brows over those haunted blue eyes.
'I think, after last night, that any sort of friendship
between the two of us, even on a superficial level, is out
of the question, don't you?'

'You really don't want to know what I'm thinking
right now!'

'Oh, I think I could take a good guess,' she jeered
coolly.

Half of Sin wanted to throttle her for her coolness
towards him this morning—and the other half of him
wanted to pick her up and carry her back to her bed. At
least when they made love they didn't argue! Well…not
until afterwards, at least…

'Somehow I doubt that—'

'Oh, thank you so much, Wallace,' Luccy cut warmly
across Sin's barely controlled anger. She turned to smile
at the elderly butler as he came out onto the terrace with
her tea and toast, leaving Sin to stand impotently by
while Wallace poured her tea for her. 'Mmm, that's
good.' She sighed after taking her first sip, a little colour
returning to her cheeks.

Wallace looked pleased. 'Master Sin kindly has my
favourite brand imported from England once a month.'

'Really?' Luccy came back non-committally—
telling Sin that if Wallace had been trying to do a little
PR work on Sin's behalf, then he might as well have
saved his breath; Luccy was certainly not impressed by
Sin's thoughtfulness towards the elderly butler!

'I'd better go,' Sin bit out tersely.

'Before you go, Master Sin…' Wallace turned to
speak to him. 'The reason I was so long getting the tea
was because Mrs Claudia telephoned…'

Luccy's attention was caught and held as a silent

exchange seemed to take place between the two men, alerting her curiosity as to exactly who Mrs Claudia was. A girlfriend of Sin's, perhaps?

Why not? After all, Sin was a very attractive and eligible bachelor; it would be ridiculous to imagine there hadn't been a woman—or even women—in his life in the two months since they had last seen each other.

Even if the very thought of Sin intimately involved with another woman made Luccy's stomach churn anew!

She hadn't quite known what to expect from him this morning, or quite how to act towards him either, and the brief conversation they'd had certainly hadn't helped to ease her tension. Being witness to a conversation between Sin and Wallace, possibly concerning the latest women in Sin's life, certainly wasn't going to help.

'Perhaps I'll go for a brief walk in the garden and leave you two men to talk—'

'That won't be necessary, Luccy,' Sin rasped, his expression one of irritation. 'In fact, it might be better if you were to stay.' He turned to the elderly butler. 'What did she want, Wallace?'

'Sin, I really think—'

'Don't,' he advised impatiently. 'Mrs Claudia is my mother,' he added as Luccy frowned.

His mother? That had been the very last explanation Luccy had been expecting!

Not that Sin had to explain himself to her. Far from it. Just as she didn't owe him any explanations, either.

'Wallace?' he prompted.

The older man nodded. 'Well, as you know, it's your birthday at the weekend—'

'I'll be thirty-six,' Sin told Luccy dryly as she gave

him a questioning look. 'My mother isn't intending to "surprise" me with a visit, is she, Wallace?' he asked.

That was the last thing Sin needed. The very last thing, in the present circumstances. Luccy was as determined to leave as he was to make her stay, without his mother adding to the confusion!

'Not that I know of,' Wallace answered cautiously.

Too cautiously as far as Sin was concerned. 'So what did she want, Wallace?'

Wallace looked pained. 'She was enquiring as to whether you would be here or in the city for your birthday on Saturday, in order that she might have your card and gift delivered to the appropriate address.'

'And?' There was more, Sin was sure of it.

'And I explained to her that as you have a guest staying here with you at the moment, I believed—'

'Wallace!' Sin groaned before dropping wearily back down into the chair he had recently vacated.

'What is it?' Luccy asked as she looked from one man to the other, Wallace looking almost guilty, Sin sitting with his gaze raised to the heavens. 'Surely it's only natural for your mother to want to send you a card and gift for your birthday?'

Although Luccy could honestly say she wasn't sure what she was supposed to do about the event. Not that she still intended being here on Saturday, but even so…

How did one treat the birthday of one's baby's father? Somehow Luccy doubted there was a book of etiquette on the subject!

'It's natural for my mother to want to send a card and gift,' Sin answered her tetchily. 'What isn't natural— or, indeed, normal—is for me to have a guest staying here with me. I don't bring people here, Luccy. Any people. Any entertaining I do, business or otherwise, I do in the city,' he elaborated as Luccy obviously still looked puzzled.

'I see,' Luccy answered slowly.

And she did. Sin had told her yesterday, when she had questioned the bathing costume in the changing-room, that he didn't bring women here. He had obviously been telling the truth if his irritation and Wallace's look of apology were anything to go by.

Although she couldn't help wondering what Wallace had made of the fact that Sin had brought her here yesterday…

'I really am sorry, Master Sin,' the elderly butler apologised now. 'I simply didn't think…'

'No—but you can bet my mother is!' Sin grimaced at the thought of exactly what his mother was thinking!

She had been dropping broad hints about grandchildren ever since Sin's father had died ten years ago, seeming to think that would be her raison d'être now that she was a widow. Sin had been just as studiously ignoring those hints, much to his mother's annoyance.

He looked up reprovingly at Wallace. 'You do realise she's probably on the telephone right this minute instructing the pilot to fly the jet down and collect her?'

'What?' Luccy looked panicked at the mere suggestion of his mother arriving here some time later today.

'Don't worry about it,' Sin said. 'I'll give him a call in a minute and tell him to cancel that instruction.'

'In that case Mrs Claudia will be on the next available flight to New York,' Wallace predicted knowledgeably.

Sin shot him a censorious glance. 'Maybe you should have thought of that before mentioning that Luccy was staying here!'

'I have apologised, Master Sin—'

'Forget it, Wallace.' Sin waved a hand. 'She was going to find out some time soon, anyway. I would just rather it had been later than sooner!'

'Would you like me to bring a fresh pot of coffee?' the butler offered.

'Good idea.' Sin nodded. 'Luccy and I need to work out a plan of action before my mother gets here.'

As far as Luccy was concerned, implementing a 'plan of action' meant that she was definitely leaving on the first available flight back to England!

'Sin—'

'I should eat some of that toast, Luccy,' he advised. 'You're going to need all your strength for when my mother arrives.'

Luccy shook her head. 'I won't be here then—'

'Oh, yes, you will,' Sin contradicted her firmly, his expression grim.

'No.'

'Luccy, whether you like it or not, the child you're carrying is her first grandchild. You hadn't thought of that,' he pointed out as Luccy felt her face pale.

No, she most definitely hadn't thought of that! But now that Sin had pointed it out to her she was only more determined to leave before Claudia Sinclair arrived. Sin was trying to bully her into marrying him; Luccy certainly didn't need any emotional pressure from Claudia Sinclair—her baby's grandmother!—to add to that.

Luccy shook her head. 'She doesn't need to be made aware of—'

'The hell she doesn't!' Sin cut in angrily, grey eyes glittering with the emotion.

'It will only confuse the issue even further.'

'There is no confusion, Luccy,' he assured her coldly. 'The only options available to you are that you either marry me or I go for custody of the baby once it's born—and, believe me, I'll win.'

Luccy only had to look at the definite resolve on his face to know that he meant it. 'You would really do that to me?'

'I'm not doing anything to you, Luccy.' He stood up impatiently. 'What is wrong with you?' He glowered down at her. 'Hell, most women would be only too happy for the chance to marry the heir to all the Sinclair millions.'

Luccy considered him guardedly. 'And you would be happy knowing that a woman had married you only for that reason?'

'I don't seem to have any choice in the matter, do I, when that's exactly the reason you're going to marry me?' he retorted.

Luccy flinched at the vehemence in his voice. 'I don't want to marry you at all!'

'It's the whole package or nothing,' he barked. 'And I do mean nothing!'

She swallowed hard as the nausea threatened to overwhelm her. Sin meant what he said. He really meant it…

'I think it's probably best if I cancel my appointments for today and make some phone calls from here instead,' Sin told her. 'I'll be in my study if you need me.'

Luccy's mouth firmed. 'I won't.'

He paused beside her chair, eyes narrowed to silver slits. 'Don't even think about trying to leave.'

Luccy's eyes flashed as she glared up at him. 'I'm to be a prisoner here, is that it?'

'Until I have my wedding ring on your finger—yes!' he confirmed without remorse.

Luccy felt the colour drain completely from her cheeks. 'I take it I am allowed to make some telephone calls myself? I do have family and friends of my own, you know, who will be worried once they realise I didn't return to England as planned.'

'Make all the phone calls you like. I'll use the business line,' Sin offered. 'Just don't expect to be leaving here any time soon.'

Why did every conversation he and Luccy had always end up a battle? Sin wondered as he strode back into the house. Even ones that began innocuously, politely, always ended with an argument, with her strong will pitted against his equally strong one.

Why was that, when it wasn't what Sin really wanted at all?

CHAPTER ELEVEN

'THIS is very kind of you, Wallace.' Luccy smiled across the kitchen at him as she sat at the breakfast bar watching him as he prepared her a plain omelette.

'Not at all, Miss Harper-O'Neill,' he assured her briskly. 'You haven't eaten anything since you arrived yesterday,' he added with concern.

'Please call me Luccy.'

'Very well, Miss Luccy.'

Luccy squirmed on the high stool she was sitting on, not sure she was comfortable with that term of address; it made her sound as if she were already one of the Sinclair family!

She had sat alone on the terrace for several minutes after Sin had left her, guessing by the fact that Wallace didn't reappear with the pot of coffee that he must have taken it to Sin in his study instead. A fact that had been confirmed when Wallace had appeared out on the terrace, without the coffee pot, to enquire whether he could get her anything hot to eat for her breakfast.

Luccy wasn't particularly hungry, that last conversation with Sin having robbed her of any appetite. But neither did she want to spend any more time in her own company. The compromise had been that she would accompany Wallace into his kitchen while he cooked her an omelette.

'What's Sin's mother like?' She felt curious about the other woman in spite of herself. The woman who, as Sin had so bluntly pointed out, would be her baby's grandmother once it was born…

'Mrs Claudia?' A warm smile of affection lit Wallace's face. 'She's a true Southern Belle,' he added consideringly. 'Just like that woman in the movies. You know the one I mean, I'm sure. Scarlett O'Hara, that's her—without the spoilt pout,' he added quickly.

Luccy laughed. 'I was always rather taken with the feisty Scarlett!'

Wallace nodded. 'Everyone loves Mrs Claudia.'

'Including Sin?' Luccy prompted curiously.

'Of course.' The butler nodded as he brought over the fluffy omelette on a plate and placed it in front of her. 'Although that doesn't mean he gives in to her. Certainly not. Master Sin has a definite mind of his own,' he said affectionately.

'Tell me about it!' Luccy muttered as she began to eat the omelette, finding that she had an appetite after all.

Wallace regarded her quizzically. 'He was only twenty-six when his father died, you know. Not very old to have taken on the mantle of something as big as Sinclair Industries, I'm sure you'll agree?'

'But I thought his grandfather…?'

'Oh, Mr Jacob kept a steady hand on the tiller,' Wallace agreed. 'But he was seventy himself at the time, and the death of his only son affected him very deeply, as you can imagine. It was left to Master Sin to carry most of the load, then and since.'

Luccy wasn't sure she really wanted to hear any of this. The last thing she wanted to do was to start admiring Sin as well as loving him!

'Of course, some people saw his youth as a weakness, and tried to take advantage of it,' Wallace continued with a frown.

Like that female employee of Sinclair Industries who had thought sleeping with the boss was a sure-fire way of attaining promotion…

She gave a rueful smile. 'You're very proud of Sin, aren't you, Wallace?'

'As if he were my own son,' he answered immediately. 'Like the son I should have had, but—well…it wasn't to be, I'm afraid,' he added with husky regret.

Luccy could hear the emotional tremor in his voice, and she could see the sadness in his eyes.

Wallace should have had a son?

Sin tried to settle down to work once he reached his study, dealing with several phone calls, including the one to his mother. As expected she was making plans to fly to New York, supposedly for his birthday on Saturday and some shopping she wanted to do in New York, but assuring him that she intended staying in the city with Jacob rather than here with him.

Sin supposed he should be grateful for small mercies; despite what he might have said to Luccy earlier, he knew it would not be a good idea to have his mother and Luccy in the same house until things were more settled.

If they ever were!

If breakfast this morning was anything to go by, they could still be fighting in twenty years' time, about everything and anything…

The two of them making love again last night probably hadn't helped, Sin acknowledged as he sat behind his desk staring broodingly out the window once he had finished making his phone calls. He and Luccy would have to call some sort of truce, at least, because this constant contention between them couldn't continue throughout the rest of her pregnancy.

Luccy wanted to leave and return to her life in England.

Sin was just as determined that she wouldn't.

Was it just about the baby?

Was any of this about the baby?

Sin became suddenly still. Was it just about the baby? Or was it—now that he had seen Luccy again, spent time with her, made love with her—that he wasn't willing to let *her* go?

Damn it, she had used him two months ago. Had seen a bigger chance for herself when she had recognised him in the restaurant that evening—

Yet he only had Paul Bridger's word for that. Luccy still vehemently denied those accusations.

Then what reason did she have for making love with him that night two months ago?

Because, like him, she had wanted to, had wanted *him*?

That was a possibility Sin hadn't even considered after she'd disappeared so suddenly that night!

Luccy claimed she had left because she'd been embarrassed by what had happened.

No, maybe he should stop thinking in those terms. Maybe Luccy wasn't *claiming* anything. Maybe she was just telling the truth?

He stood up abruptly. He needed to talk to Luccy.

Not argue with her. Not threaten her. Not make love with her. Just talk to her.

'What happened?' Luccy prompted Wallace gently.

He smiled sadly. 'I was young and foolish, invincible as only the very young believe themselves to be. I wanted it all. My career in the army. My wife and future child with me when I was posted overseas.'

Luccy wasn't surprised this man had once been in the army; there was something about the way he walked, his bearing, that indicated he had been in the military.

She stood up to pour some coffee into a second mug, silently placing it in front of him as she resumed her own seat to look at him encouragingly. Wallace didn't give the impression he was a man who talked about his personal life very often. If at all.

Wallace absently took a sip of the coffee. 'My wife didn't want to come with me that last time. She—she was five months pregnant, and didn't think it was safe for the baby. She was right,' Wallace told Luccy abruptly. 'They both died.'

Sin had gone out onto the terrace looking for Luccy, and when he couldn't find her either there or in her bedroom he went in search of Wallace to see if he knew where she had gone, half of him fearing that she had decided to leave, after all, despite him telling her not to.

He came to a stunned halt outside the kitchen door as he overheard part of the conversation between Luccy and Wallace. A conversation Sin knew he had no right to interrupt once he realised what the two of them were talking about.

He had known Wallace for years. Respected him.

Loved him like a member of his own family. And yet he had never known that Wallace had once had a wife, let alone that she had been expecting his child.

He should go, leave them to it, and yet something made Sin stay…

'I'm sure that wasn't your fault,' Luccy assured him.

'Not directly, no,' Wallace confirmed ruefully. 'But if I hadn't insisted that she come with me—' He broke off, shaking his head. 'We had gone out for the day, and she—Rebecca went into labour too early. We were miles from the nearest hospital, and when I did finally manage to get her to one the facilities were poor, the hospital overcrowded, and the staff were rushed off their feet trying to deal with it all. A woman about to give birth didn't seem like a priority to them. It happened every day. Was nothing to worry about, they told me.'

'Usually it isn't,' Luccy sympathised.

'No.' Wallace sighed. 'The baby had the cord around its neck, though, was already dead, and Rebecca haemorrhaged and died, too, before any of us realised what was happening.'

Luccy reached out to clasp his hand with her own. 'There was nothing you could have done.'

He looked up at her. 'I could have listened to Rebecca in the first place when she told me she wanted to have the baby at home, where she could be within easy reach of a hospital and be near her family. The least I could have done was listen to what she wanted,' he concluded emotionally.

As Sin should listen to Luccy when she told him she didn't want to be here with him?

Oh, not because he feared that something might

happen to her or the baby if he forced her to stay—he would do his damnedest to ensure that didn't happen, no matter what the circumstances of their own relationship. But maybe he didn't have the right to make her stay here simply because it wasn't what *Luccy* wanted…?

The fact that Wallace had felt comfortable enough with Luccy, after only knowing her a few hours, to confide something in her that he had told none of the Sinclair family only added to Sin's earlier doubts.

Maybe it was time *he* listened to Luccy…

Maybe it was time he more than listened to her!

'You're very quiet this evening?' Luccy looked uncertainly across the dinner table at Sin as he sat opposite her so broodingly silent, only playing with the dessert—as he had only picked at the two previous courses, too—that Wallace had just served at the end of a meal that had been eaten almost in silence.

Luccy didn't count comments about the pleasantness of the evening as conversation!

She hadn't really seen much of Sin throughout the day as he'd stayed closeted in his study, but Wallace had more than made up for Sin's absence, the two of them having fallen into an easy friendship, Luccy choosing to relax and eat her lunch in the kitchen with the older man, too.

The feeling of relaxation had come to an abrupt halt the moment Sin had joined her outside for dinner, once again looking devastatingly handsome in a black evening suit and snowy white shirt, the darkness of his hair still damp from the shower.

Sin drew in a sharp breath. 'Luccy, if you could do what you wanted, exactly what you wanted, what would it be?'

She eyed him frowningly. 'Is this a trick question? You know, another excuse, yet another reason, to hurl accusations at me?'

Sin knew that he thoroughly deserved that remark. 'No,' he sighed. 'No tricks. No accusations. I just want a straightforward answer to a straightforward question.'

'Oh.'

Sin gave a rueful smile at her obvious surprise. 'I promise not to use your answer against you.'

Luccy still eyed him warily. He had been in a strange mood all evening. Their present conversation was even stranger. 'Well…' she took her time about answering '…obviously I would like to go home to England as soon as possible.'

'Obviously,' Sin acknowledged dryly.

'Then I suppose I would like to go on working until the baby is born—'

'For PAN Cosmetics?'

'No, I don't think so.' She grimaced.

'Why the hell not?' Sin frowned darkly. 'What?' he prompted with a scowl as Luccy looked across at him expectantly.

She shrugged. 'I was waiting for you to add, "You certainly wanted another contract with them badly enough two months ago to sleep with me"!'

Sin sat back in his chair, his face partly in shadow. 'I said no tricks and no accusations, remember?'

Of course Luccy remembered, but that didn't mean she hadn't expected the odd insult from him. 'Okay.' She nodded. 'Then, no, I don't want to work for PAN Cosmetics once my current contract is at an end.'

'Because I own it?'

'Partly,' Luccy confirmed ruefully. 'But mainly

because it's too big a commitment to make when I'll have a baby to look after—'

'You don't have to take care of the baby yourself,' Sin interjected.

'What if I want to?'

'Do you?'

'As it happens—yes!' she told him slightly indignantly. 'I'm sure that in your world children are brought up by nannies, but not in mine! Any work that I do in future will have to be fitted in around the baby's needs.'

Sin was getting much more than he had bargained for when he'd opened this conversation! He had expected Luccy to want to go home to England. He had even known, if it was left to her, that he would play no part in what happened after that. What he hadn't expected was that she would sacrifice her commitment to her career in order to care for the baby herself...

'Don't worry, Sin, I wouldn't expect you to keep me or the baby in luxury or otherwise!' she added scornfully. 'I would try to keep enough work going for us to be able to survive without that.'

To survive.

He didn't want Luccy or his child to just survive!

'And how do you think our son or daughter would feel about that when they were old enough to realise that their father could have made life so much easier for you both?'

Her chin rose challengingly. 'I hope that they will have learnt to respect me enough to know that I did what I thought was right.'

To Sin it was like having the blinkers he had worn for the last two months, since Luccy had left the hotel so abruptly that night and he had listened to what Paul

Bridger had had to say about her a couple of days later, suddenly fall from his eyes.

Given a choice, Luccy was determined to do what was right for the baby as well as her.

And she obviously didn't believe having Sin in their lives was right for either of them...

Who could blame her?

Certainly not Sin.

He had accused her of blackmail. Not just over that night at the hotel, but about the baby too. God, no wonder she hated the very sight of him!

He didn't like himself very much at that moment, either...

'What if a contract with PAN could be worked out to fit in around your work schedule?'

'Sin, you're talking about this as if it really were a possibility rather than just hypothetical.' She frowned her confusion.

'Maybe it is.'

Luccy looked at him searchingly. Did he really mean it? After all that had happened, after all the things Sin had said, was he going to let her go after all?

If so, where was the elation, the feeling of freedom she had expected to feel?

Because Luccy didn't feel either of those things. What she felt was a deep sense of let-down, an even greater heaviness at the possibility of not having Sin as part of her life.

She had realised last night that she was actually in love with Sin, had even begun to hope, she also now realised, in a secret corner of her heart, that if they did marry each other one day he might come to return that love.

Was he now telling her that she could go, that he didn't want her or their baby?

'You said it yourself last night, Luccy, this isn't going to work,' he said abruptly, throwing his napkin down onto the table top as he stood up.

'It isn't?'

'No,' he rasped. 'I've decided I don't want to spend the next few decades married to a woman who hates me.'

'But—'

'First thing in the morning I'll make the arrangements for you to fly back to England on the first available flight.'

'I'm more than capable of making my own arrangements.'

'I know you're more than capable of doing anything you set your mind to, Luccy,' Sin bit out, his eyes glacial. 'I *want* to do it, okay?'

So that he could be absolutely sure she had gone? Luccy wondered numbly.

Was this it, then? After all the suspicion, all the accusations, and all the arguments, now that Sin had decided he didn't want her was he putting her out of his life, sending her back to England as quickly as possible?

For a moment Luccy felt a fierce shaft of pain in her chest, as if her heart were actually breaking, and then the numbness took over, pervading every part of her, dulling that pain to just a nagging ache.

It was over.

Sin was giving her exactly what she had said she wanted.

To go back to England.

To bring the baby up on her own.

When the only thing that Luccy really wanted, the only thing that really mattered to her—Sin himself—she could never have.

'Fine.' She rose slowly to her feet. 'I—you'll give me chance to say goodbye to Wallace before I go?'

'Of course.' Sin's mouth twisted self-derisively as he acknowledged that Luccy had grown more fond of Wallace in the last twenty-four hours than she had of him in the months since they had first met.

She looked very pale in the moonlight, almost ghostly, her white knee-length dress adding to that illusion. Sin's hands clenched into fists at his sides as he acknowledged that this was probably the last time he would be alone with her like this.

Damn it, self-sacrifice had never been a part of his nature!

But neither was forcing someone else's will to his own.

He didn't want to let Luccy go. He was only doing it because he knew he had no other choice...

Maybe once Luccy returned to England, once she felt back in control of her own life, he could—they could—

He was deluding himself now. Luccy didn't want him in her life. Not now. Not ever.

Then he frowned. 'I expected you to look a lot happier than this.'

'Did you?' she returned dully. 'Maybe I don't quite trust that it's happening yet?'

'No,' Sin accepted dryly. 'I'm sure once the plane takes off tomorrow that the relief will kick in!'

Luccy was equally sure that once she even stepped onto that plane tomorrow she was going to feel as if her heart had been ripped right out of her body! She certainly wouldn't be taking it with her...

She bit her bottom lip to stop it trembling as the numbness began to crack under the strain, allowing the pain to increase to an almost unbearable pitch. 'I presume you will still want access once the baby is born?'

He nodded. 'Let me know the name of your lawyer when you get home and I'll have my own lawyer contact him or her so they can sort out the details.'

Luccy swallowed down the lump that had risen in her throat. Sin was so calm. So businesslike. So cold...

'Just for the baby. I won't be needing anything from you for myself—'

'The lawyers will work out the details, Luccy,' he repeated harshly.

What exactly did that mean? If Sin thought she was still only interested in what she could get out of him, then—

Leave it, Luccy, she told herself firmly. If there was anything in the agreement that she didn't like then she could always refuse to sign it. It might even serve to convince Sin that she really wasn't what he thought she was. Maybe...

'Very well.' Luccy managed a dignified nod of her head before she turned to leave, a part of her still hoping that he would stop her, that he would call out, tell her—

Tell her what? That he loved her as she loved him?

How could Sin possibly do that when he didn't love her?

'Luccy?'

'Yes?' She turned back sharply, Sin just a blur in the moonlight through the tears she was trying to stop from falling.

'I'm sorry things didn't work out.'

Luccy gave an abrupt nod before turning away, too

distraught to speak, and knowing that the trembling of her voice would give her away if she attempted to do so.

Tomorrow she was going home.

And the only home she wanted, the only home she would ever want, was with Sin, wherever he might be…

CHAPTER TWELVE

'MASTER SIN...?'

Sin looked up, grateful for Wallace's interruption from the papers he had been staring at for the last ten minutes or so since coming to his study but not actually managed to read a word of. 'Yes, Wallace?' He managed a strained smile.

The butler frowned. 'I thought you might be interested to know that Miss Luccy has gone.'

Sin frowned darkly. 'What do you mean—gone?'

'Gone as in gone, Master Sin.' The older man grimaced. 'I took a morning cup of tea to her bedroom just now only to find the room empty and all of her clothes gone from the drawers and wardrobe—I can assure you I am not mistaken, Master Sin,' he added as Sin stood up as if to go and check for himself. 'She left a note...'

'A note?' Sin repeated dully, an icy shiver running down the length of his spine.

Luccy hadn't been present at breakfast earlier, but Sin had assumed—

'Let me see it,' he rasped grimly, holding out his hand.

Wallace's brows rose. 'The note wasn't addressed to *you*, Master Sin...'

'Then who—*you*?' Sin said woodenly even as he dropped back down into the chair behind his desk.

Luccy had gone and she hadn't even bothered to say goodbye to him!

Luccy had *gone*.

It was all Sin could think of. All that seemed important.

Why, when he had told her that he would book her flight back to England today—when he had booked her on a flight later today—hadn't she waited for him to drive her to the airport and at least let them say goodbye properly?

Luccy was actually strapped in her seat, the doors locked ready for take off, when she heard the engines being switched off, her heart plummeting as the flight attendant came on the tannoy to announce there would be a short but unavoidable delay to their departure.

The elderly woman beside Luccy looked as if she might be about to launch into a conversation, probably about the inconsideration of the airline, which was more than enough incentive for Luccy to rest her head back on the seat and close her eyes.

She didn't feel like talking to anyone right now!

It had been much more complicated getting away from Sin's house earlier this morning than she had hoped, organising a taxi to pick her up made more difficult by the fact that it couldn't be admitted to the house without the driver first speaking to Wallace on the intercom, and so instantly alerting the butler to her departure. And once Wallace knew he would no doubt inform Sin...

So instead Luccy had instructed the driver to wait for

her on the other side of the security gates, and simply walked down the driveway with her bags. All the time feeling like some sort of criminal making a getaway from the scene!

But the alternative, waiting for Sin to drive her to the airport later today, was even more unthinkable, the mere thought of having to actually say goodbye to him enough to make her feel ill.

She—

'Luccy.'

Her lids flew wide as she recognised that voice, feeling completely disoriented as she stared up at Sin as he stood in the aisle beside her seat looking so arrogantly confident.

But he couldn't be here! She had to be hallucinating—

'Time to go, Luccy,' he prompted huskily as he held out his hand to her.

'I—but—what are you doing here?' she muttered as she became aware of the gazes of the other passengers fixed on the two of them. Some of them just looked curious, but others definitely looked furious that she was obviously the one who had caused this delay in their departure. The woman sitting beside Luccy was unashamedly listening to their conversation.

Sin eyed Luccy quizzically. 'What does it look like I'm doing?' he murmured.

Luccy frowned. It looked as if he was waiting for her to accompany him off the plane. But why was he? What possible reason could he have for subjecting them both to this further embarrassment? He should have just been glad that she had gone!

She swallowed hard. 'You told me to leave—'

'I said you *could* leave.'

'Same thing.'

'Not exactly,' he chided. 'I certainly didn't expect you to go without so much as a goodbye,' he added grimly.

'I—' Luccy glared at him frustratedly. 'This is ridiculous! You *told* me to go.'

His mouth tightened. 'I've changed my mind.'

Luccy had never felt so flustered in her life. How had Sin even got on the plane, for goodness' sake? The flight attendant had already announced that all the passengers and luggage were on board. Everyone had their seat belts on. The engines had been roaring ready for taxiing to the runway.

Damn it, she had been so close to getting away without having to see Sin again!

Damn him!

He had no right to just turn up here.

She still couldn't believe he had actually delayed— no, *stopped* the flight, in order to come on board!

'Well, I haven't changed mine,' she assured him firmly.

'Luccy, the sooner you get off the plane, the quicker these people will be able to continue with their flight.' The softness of Sin's tone didn't conceal its steely edge.

'You're not being fair now!' Luccy glared at him.

Sin had broken every speed limit on his way to the airport, only to arrive and realise that he was still too late, that Luccy was already on the plane waiting to leave.

One look at her face now told him that she wasn't inclined to get off again, either!

Not that Sin could exactly blame her. He had told her she could leave. He just hadn't expected that she would leave without seeing him again, without so much as a goodbye.

'I never claimed to be fair,' he drawled ruefully.

'You—'

'Look, love, I'd get off the plane with him, if I were you,' the elderly woman seated beside Luccy interrupted their conversation. 'He doesn't look like the type of man that you argue with. That you would want to argue with,' she added with a coy glance in Sin's direction.

A glance Luccy took exception to as she fumed quietly to herself. She still had no idea how he had got onto this flight in the first place, although no doubt it had something to do with the influence of the Sinclair name—and their billions.

'I'm going home,' Luccy told him determinedly.

He nodded. 'You have a seat booked on another flight that leaves in five hours' time.'

Luccy eyed him suspiciously. But of course he had her booked onto another flight later today. Just as he had said that he would.

She had left earlier in the hopes of avoiding any more conversation with Sin, but she could see by the determination of his expression that was no longer possible. And these poor people on the plane had been delayed long enough already…

Luccy undid her seat belt and stood up. 'What about my luggage?'

'Already taken off and in the car,' Sin dismissed as he stepped back so that she could move into the aisle in front of him.

Of course it was. Why had she ever doubted it?

'Good luck, love,' the elderly lady called after her as Luccy walked down the gangway to where the door stood open waiting for them to leave.

Luck?

Luccy was going to need a lot more than luck if she was going to get through another conversation with Sin without breaking down…

'You'll give yourself jaw ache if you don't relax soon,' Sin murmured soothingly. Luccy was sitting absolutely silently beside him in his car as he drove the two of them away from the airport.

'I would like to give *you* jaw ache!' she muttered, dark sunglasses hiding the emotion in her eyes. 'Half those people on the plane probably think I'm some sort of criminal being carted off to the police station!'

'Then they would be wrong.'

'You made me feel like a criminal!' Luccy burst out angrily, her silence obviously at an end.

'I didn't mean to.'

'I have no idea how you managed to delay the flight, let alone get onto the plane.' She gave a snort of disgust. 'You probably own shares in the airline—'

'Make that a lot of shares,' Sin interjected quietly.

Luccy's fingernails dug into the shoulder bag she was holding protectively on her knees. 'You think the Sinclair name gives you the right to do exactly as you please, don't you?'

'No.'

'Well, let me tell you that I don't give that—' she gave a dismissive snap of her fingers '—for the Sinclair name or the Sinclair *trillions*! You're—'

'I know.'

'—nothing but a—a— What did you say?' Luccy turned to look at him dazedly.

Sin's mouth tightened. 'I said I know, Luccy,' he acknowledged heavily.

Her brows rose. 'What do you know?'

'That you don't give a damn for the Sinclair name or the Sinclair wealth.'

'You—you know that, do you?'

'I believe so, yes.'

'But I—how do you know that? Last night—'

'Luccy, I would really rather we weren't involved in an accident before we get back to the house,' he cut in. 'So do you think we could have the rest of this conversation once we get back?'

Luccy looked at him searchingly, noting the grimness of his expression, the nerve pulsing in his own tightly clenched jaw. He looked—she wasn't sure how he looked!

She wasn't exactly sure about the state of her own emotions, if she were honest. She had been stunned when she'd first looked up and seen Sin standing beside her seat on the plane. Had been mortified at how he'd drawn attention to her in that embarrassing way. But another part of her—another part of her had leapt with joy at his being there! Had begun to hope—

Hope what?

That Sin had come after her because he actually cared for her?

That really would be allowing herself to wander into the realms of fantasy.

Then what was Sin doing here?

He had changed his mind about letting her go, he had said. But what did that mean? The fact that Sin had booked her a seat on a flight later today meant that she really shouldn't read too much into that statement…

But she wanted to!

Oh, how she wanted to!

'Would you like something to drink?' Sin offered

politely when they were once more on the terrace over-looking parkland.

Luccy tapped her foot impatiently against one of the concrete slabs. 'What I would like, as soon as you have said what it is you want to say, is to be on my flight back to England!'

Sin looked at her, seeing her face pale beneath those dark sunglasses. 'Why did you leave without saying goodbye?'

A little colour entered her cheeks. 'I left Wallace a note.'

'So he told me.' A nerve pulsed in Sin's tightly clenched jaw as he recalled that Luccy had felt the need to say goodbye to Wallace but not to him.

She gave a dismissive shrug. 'After last night there didn't seem to be anything left for the two of us to say to each other.'

Sin drew in a sharp breath. 'Luccy, do you have any idea why I decided I had to let you go, after all?'

She looked at him uncertainly. 'Because you didn't want to spend the next few decades married to a woman who hates you was, I believe, the reason you gave me?'

Sin frowned. '*Do* you hate me, Luccy?'

'You said I did.'

'I'm more interested in what *you* have to say than anything I may or may not have said!' he rasped.

Luccy eyed him, still not sure what he wanted from her. Or how much more of this she could take...

She had left in the way she had in order to avoid another scene like this, had no defences left, against her love for him, or the way she was still so physically aware of him as he stood there so tall and handsome in his black polo shirt and faded blue jeans.

'What do you want from me, Sin?' She gave a pained frown, her hands tightly clasped together in front of her.

'I want—' He broke off, giving a frustrated shake of his head. 'What happened between the two of us two months ago, Luccy?'

She drew in a ragged breath. 'I thought you were the one with all the answers on that subject.'

She had never done anything as reckless in her life before as going off with someone as she had done with Sin that night. She'd never do anything like it again, either!

Her eyes widened as Sin walked slowly, determinedly, towards her, not sure she could keep her fragile barriers in place if he came too close to her.

And then he was close to her, very close, so close that Luccy could no longer breathe…

'I don't have the answer to that one.' He looked down at her. 'You knocked me off my feet that night, do you know that?'

'No…' she breathed, her gaze caught and held by his.

'Totally.' Sin nodded. 'And then when I came out of the shower and found you gone…' He gave another shake of his head. 'It was almost as if I had imagined you.'

Luccy grimaced. 'I have nightmares like that too sometimes.' Sin smiled slightly. 'You were no nightmare, Luccy. The nightmare only began after I spoke to Paul Bridger,' he grated, his mouth tightening at the memory.

'When you chose to believe Paul's version of what had happened that night instead of mine, you mean!' Luccy reminded him sharply.

Sin closed his eyes briefly before opening them again. 'He lied, didn't he, Luccy? Every word he said was a damned lie!'

'Yes, it was a lie,' she confirmed slowly. 'But how do you know that? Have you spoken to him again?'

Sin's hands clenched at his sides as he saw the truth—belatedly—shining in her candid blue eyes. 'I was angry and confused that night; I really couldn't understand why you left when we had shared something so beautiful.' He drew in a ragged breath. 'Luccy, I've been allowing something that happened in my past, along with Bridger's lies, to influence my reasoning,' he admitted. 'And, despite your denials, until yesterday I've continued to allow the past to influence me.'

'Yesterday? What happened yesterday? Did you speak to Paul Bridger then?'

'I haven't spoken to anyone,' he said. 'I have several things I would like to say to him! But, no, Luccy, I didn't need to speak to anyone yesterday to know that you've been telling me the truth all along.'

'So you no longer believe that I coldly, calculatedly made love with you?'

He grimaced. 'I know you didn't.'

Luccy looked dazed. 'I've never behaved like that before, Sin. Never. It was completely out of character for me.' She shook her head. 'I didn't even understand it myself until I realised—' She broke off abruptly.

'Until you realised what, Luccy?' Sin prompted huskily.

Her chin rose. 'You want me to bare my soul completely, is that it, Sin?' she choked. 'Want me to tell you that I've only ever had one other sexual experience, a horrible fumbling night years ago that I never wanted to repeat? Want me to tell you that when we made love it was—it was out of this world? Unbelievable? Everything

I had ever thought—hoped—it could be? Is this what you want from me, Sin?' she challenged emotionally.

Sin reached out and touched Luccy's cheek, gently, caressingly, her beauty such that she completely took his breath away. 'Luccy, will you marry me?' he whispered.

'Wh—what…?'

Sin swallowed hard before repeating the question, a little louder this time. 'Will you marry me, Luccy?'

Luccy took a step back even as she eyed him suspiciously. 'You haven't finished explaining why you were sending me away.'

'I decided I had to let you go if that was what you really wanted. That isn't the same as sending you away.'

No, it wasn't, was it…?

'Do you want to leave, Luccy?' Sin looked at her intently.

Of course she didn't want to leave. Not if there was a chance the two of them could—

She was being ridiculous again! So Sin was starting to have doubts about Paul Bridger's version of things—what did that prove? It certainly didn't mean that Sin loved her in the way that she loved him. Or that he ever would!

She nodded. 'I think it's best for everyone, don't you?'

A nerve pulsed in his jaw. 'Not for me.'

'Sin, you can't marry me just because I'm expecting your baby. I've already explained to you—told you—why I can't marry you for that reason, either,' she reminded him shakily.

Sin reached out and grasped her arms. 'What if I'm not asking you to marry me just because you're pregnant?'

'But you are—aren't you?'

He drew in a ragged breath, knowing too much depended on his answer for him not to tell Luccy the truth. If she still turned him down afterwards— He didn't even want to think about that!

'I love you, Luccy,' he rasped. 'I love you, damn it!' he repeated determinedly. 'So much that the thought of you leaving—going back to England and leaving me, now or any time in the future—is killing me!'

Luccy stared up at him, totally stunned. Had Sin really just said—? Had he really just told her—?

She gave a jerky shake of her head. 'You can't love me!'

Sin gave a humourless smile. 'Maybe you'll believe me if I tell you that whether you marry me or not I intend spending the rest of my life showing you just how much I love you. I won't let you go, Luccy, not if it takes me fifty years to convince you!'

He meant it. He really meant it!

Sin loved her.

Luccy looked up at him, able to see the sincerity of that love burning in his eyes, accompanied by an expression of uncertainty that was totally alien to his nature...

She took a deep breath. 'I fell in love with you that very first night, Sin. That was what I realised that night at the hotel,' she finished her earlier sentence for him. 'And I left so suddenly because that realisation terrified the life out of me!'

It was the first time that Luccy had actually admitted that truth to herself.

She had fallen in love with Sin almost on sight.

That was the reason she had behaved so—so impetuously.

And she loved him still!

Her eyes glowed with the emotion. 'I love you, Sin. I was only leaving today because I love you. Because I couldn't bear the thought of being with you and not having you love me in return!'

His answer was to sweep her up in his arms as his mouth fiercely claimed hers.

It was some time later before either of them could put a coherent sentence together, Luccy snuggled in Sin's arms as they sat together on the sofa in the sitting-room.

Luccy chuckled softly. 'I still can't believe you stopped the plane taking off.'

Sin's arms tightened about her. 'I would have bought the whole damned airline if I had to.'

'That's going to take a bit of getting used to…'

Sin looked down at her curiously. 'What is?'

She shrugged. 'Being married to a man who could buy out an airline if he wanted to.' She grimaced. 'I come from a very ordinary background, Sin. Wonderful, but ordinary. What if—?'

'I sincerely hope you aren't having doubts about marrying me because I'm *rich*?' Sin frowned fiercely.

Luccy winced. 'It could be something of a problem, yes.' She shook her head. 'Your family is going to think you've gone totally insane marrying a nobody like me.'

'You aren't a nobody, and my family are going to love you,' Sin assured her indulgently. 'As I love you.' He sobered. 'Please will you marry me, Luccy?' Sin repeated gruffly as he held her tightly against him.

She eyed him uncertainly. 'You're really sure it's what you want?'

'I'm absolutely positive it's what I want. In fact, I'm not settling for anything less!' His arms tightened about her. 'Hurry up and give me your answer, Luccy—before Wallace gets tired of waiting in the kitchen and comes in here and does my proposing for me,' he added teasingly.

Luccy laughed happily. 'I think Wallace likes me.'

'Not as much as I do,' Sin assured her, his gaze intent on her face. 'I appreciate what happened to your sister must be a concern for you, Luccy, but you won't ever have need to doubt me or my love for you. I promise I will love you for the rest of my life,' he vowed.

This really wasn't the same as Abby, Luccy realised ruefully. Her sister had only been eighteen years old when she became pregnant, and Rory had only been nineteen. They had both been so young, too young, to have the responsibility of a baby as well as marriage thrust upon them so suddenly...

Luccy looked up at Sin, knowing that she didn't doubt him or their future together. How could she when she could see the love shining in his eyes for her, could feel it in the strength of his arms as he held her as if he never wanted to let her go?

'I will marry you and I promise to love you for the rest of my life,' she returned emotionally.

A smile lit his face. 'Then we can't fail to be happy together!'

No, they wouldn't fail. Luccy was absolutely sure of it.

CHAPTER THIRTEEN

'I WAS only joking when I made that rash remark about carrying your camera equipment for you when they wheeled you into the delivery room.' Sin frowned worriedly as he sat beside the bed where Luccy lay briefly at rest after a contraction.

Luccy gave him a reassuring smile. 'How was I to know the twins would decide they wanted to be born earlier than expected?'

Twins.

They had learnt when they had attended the first scan that Luccy was expecting, not one baby, but two. It had been a shock, but not an unpleasant one.

But they certainly hadn't expected Luccy to go into labour at only thirty-six weeks. Luccy had actually been out on the last photographic shoot she had scheduled before the birth when she'd telephoned Sin and asked him to come and get her. And quickly, if he didn't want to miss the birth!

'I hate seeing you in pain!' Sin looked very pale, his eyes dark with worry, lines of strain beside his nose and mouth.

They had been married for five and a half months

now. Five and a half months of absolute bliss, when their love for each other had just grown stronger and stronger. And Sin had been right about his family; they did love her.

Luccy gave Sin's hand a squeeze. 'It's going to be fine,' she reassured him huskily.

He shook his head. 'I would never have put you through this if I had realised how much pain you were going to be in!'

She gave him a teasing look. 'I don't think either you or I had much choice in the matter, remember?'

Sin looked down at her searchingly. 'Do you regret—?'

'I don't regret a single thing, Sin,' she interrupted him firmly. 'Not one single moment of our life together.'

'If anything should happen to you—'

'It isn't going to,' she promised softly. 'Really, Sin. A couple of hours, and you'll forget about all of this.'

'A couple of hours!' Sin almost went green at the thought.

'You'll see.' She nodded, her fingers tightening about his as she felt the beginning of another contraction. 'Uh oh, here we go again!'

Sin wasn't sure how he survived the next gut-wrenching hour, let alone Luccy, as there was nothing more he could do than hold her hand and watch as she writhed with pain. He certainly loved Luccy too much to ever put her through this again! It was the most excruciating, heart-aching—

'Your daughter, Mr Sinclair.'

Sin looked down dazedly at the blanket-wrapped bundle that was placed into his arms while Luccy and the doctor and nurses concentrated on bringing his son into the world too.

The baby looked so tiny, so fragile, so absolutely beautiful! She had Luccy's black hair, with a soft creamy brow, the silkiest lashes resting against her rounded cheek, a button of a nose, and a tiny rosebud of a mouth.

'Oh…' Sin gave the softest of gasps as those silky lashes swept upwards and he found himself falling in love for the second time in his life as looked into deep blue eyes.

His daughter.

Luccy and Sin's daughter.

Claudia Anne. Claudia for Sin's mother. Anne for Luccy's.

'And your son.' Only minutes later the midwife stood beside him holding out a second bundle.

Sin shifted Claudia slightly in his arms to accommodate her brother.

Another shock of dark hair, a creamy soft brow, button nose and tiny rosebud mouth, but this time the baby's eyes were already open and looking up at him.

Sin's heart melted completely as he looked down at his son.

Luccy and Sin's son.

Jacob Henry Sinclair.

Jacob for Sin's father and grandfather, Henry for Luccy's.

'Feeling better now?'

Sin gave a choked laugh as he turned to look at a tired but obviously ecstatically happy Luccy. 'Am I feeling better?' He stood up to place Claudia into her waiting arms. 'Meet our daughter, my love.'

Luccy looked down at the tiny but perfect baby she held in her arms. 'She's so beautiful, Sin,' she choked.

'And our son.' Sin placed Jacob in her other arm. 'Thank you, Luccy.' He gazed lovingly at his family.

Luccy looked up to return his smile. 'Thank you.'
'I love you.'
'I love you, too.'
It was all that mattered.
All that would ever matter...

* * * * *

Turn the page for an exclusive extract from

THE PLAYBOY SHEIKH'S VIRGIN STABLE-GIRL
by
Sharon Kendrick

Claimed by the sheikh—for her innocence!

Polo-playing Sheikh Prince Kaliq Al'Farisi loves his women as much as his horses. They're wild, willing and he's their master!

Stable girl Eleni is a local Calistan girl. Raised by her brutal father on the horse racing circuit, she feels unlovable. When her precious horses are given to Sheikh Kaliq she *refuses* to be parted from them.

The playboy sheikh is determined to bed her, and when he realizes she's a virgin the challenge only becomes more interesting. However, Kaliq is torn; his body wants Eleni, yet his heart wants to protect her....

"WHAT WOULD YOU SAY, MY DAUGHTER, if I told you that a royal prince was coming to the home of your father?"

She would say that he *had* been drinking, after all. But never to his face, of course. If Papa was having one of his frequent flights of fancy then it was always best to play along with it.

Eleni kept her face poker-straight. "A royal prince, Papa?" she questioned gravely.

"Yes, indeed!" He pushed his face forward. "The Prince Kaliq Al'Farisi," he crowed, "is coming to my house to play cards with me!"

Her father had gone insane! These were ideas of grandeur run riot! And what was Eleni to do? What if he continued to make such idle boasts in front of the men who were sitting waiting to begin the long night of card-playing? Surely that would make him a laughingstock and ruin what little reputation he had left.

"Papa," she whispered urgently, "I beg you to think clearly. What place would a royal prince have *here?*"

But she was destined never to hear a reply, even though his mouth had opened like a puppet's, for there came the sound of distant hooves. The steady, powerful thud of horses as they thundered over the parched sands. On the still, thick air the muffled beat grew closer and louder until it filled Eleni's ears like the sound of the desert wolves that howled at the silver moon when it was at its fullest.

Toward them galloped a clutch of four horses, and as Eleni watched, one of them broke free and surged forward like a black stream of oil gushing out of the arid sand. For a moment, she stood there, transfixed—for this was as beautiful and as reckless a piece of riding as she had ever witnessed.

Illuminated by the orange-gold of the dying sun, she saw a colossus of a man with an ebony stallion between his thighs that he urged on with a joyful shout. The man's bare head was as dark as the horse he rode and his skin gleamed like some bright and burnished metal. Robes of pure silk clung to the hard sinews of his body. As he approached, Eleni could see a face so forbidding that some deep-rooted fear made her wonder if he had the power to turn to dust all those who stood before him.

And a face so inherently beautiful that it was as if all the desert flowers had bloomed at once.

It was then that Eleni understood the full and daunting truth. Her father's bragging *had* been true, and riding toward their humble abode was indeed Prince Kaliq Al'Farisi. Kaliq the daredevil, the lover of women, the playboy, the gambler and irresponsible twin son of Prince Ashraf. The man it was said could make women moan with pleasure simply by looking at them.

She had not seen him since she was a young girl in the crowds watching the royal family pass by. Back then, he had been doing his military service and wearing the uniform of the Calistan Navy. And back then he had

been an arresting young man, barely out of his twenties.
But now—a decade and a half on—he was at the most
magnificent peak of his manhood, with a raw and beautiful masculinity that seemed to shimmer from his
muscular frame.

"By the wolves that howl!" Eleni whimpered, and
ran inside the house.

* * * * *

Be sure to look for
THE PLAYBOY SHEIKH'S VIRGIN STABLE-GIRL
by Sharon Kendrick,
available August 2009 from Harlequin Presents®!

HARLEQUIN *Presents*

TWO CROWNS, TWO ISLANDS, ONE LEGACY

*A royal family torn apart by pride and lust for power,
reunited by purity and passion*

THE ROYAL HOUSE *of* KAREDES

Pick up the next adventure in this passionate series!

Eight volumes to collect and treasure!

www.eHarlequin.com

HP12843

HARLEQUIN *Presents*

International Billionaires

*Life is a game of power and pleasure.
And these men play to win!*

BLACKMAILED INTO THE GREEK TYCOON'S BED
by **Carol Marinelli**

When ruthless billionaire Xante Rossi catches
mousy Karin red-handed, he designs a way to save
her from scandal. But she'll have to earn
the favor—in his bedroom!

Book #2846

Available August 2009

Look for the last installment of
International Billionaires from Harlequin Presents!

THE VIRGIN SECRETARY'S
IMPOSSIBLE BOSS
by Carole Mortimer
September 2009

www.eHarlequin.com

HPI2846

REQUEST YOUR FREE BOOKS!

HARLEQUIN® Presents®

PASSION
GUARANTEED
SEDUCTION

2 FREE NOVELS
PLUS 2
FREE GIFTS!

YES! Please send me 2 FREE Harlequin Presents® novels and my 2 FREE gifts (gifts are worth about $10). After receiving them, if I don't wish to receive any more books, I can return the shipping statement marked "cancel". If I don't cancel, I will receive 6 brand-new novels every month and be billed just $4.05 per book in the U.S. or $4.74 per book in Canada. That's a savings of close to 15% off the cover price! It's quite a bargain! Shipping and handling is just 50¢ per book*. I understand that accepting the 2 free books and gifts places me under no obligation to buy anything. I can always return a shipment and cancel at any time. Even if I never buy another book, the two free books and gifts are mine to keep forever.   106 HDN EYRQ 306 HDN EYR2

Name _____ (PLEASE PRINT)

Address _____ Apt. #

City _____ State/Prov. _____ Zip/Postal Code

Signature (if under 18, a parent or guardian must sign)

Mail to the **Harlequin Reader Service:**
IN U.S.A.: P.O. Box 1867, Buffalo, NY 14240-1867
IN CANADA: P.O. Box 609, Fort Erie, Ontario L2A 5X3

Not valid to current subscribers of Harlequin Presents books.

Are you a current subscriber of Harlequin Presents books and want to receive the larger-print edition? Call 1-800-873-8635 today!

* Terms and prices subject to change without notice. Prices do not include applicable taxes. Sales tax applicable in N.Y. Canadian residents will be charged applicable provincial taxes and GST. Offer not valid in Quebec. This offer is limited to one order per household. All orders subject to approval. Credit or debit balances in a customer's account(s) may be offset by any other outstanding balance owed by or to the customer. Please allow 4 to 6 weeks for delivery. Offer available while quantities last.

Your Privacy: Harlequin Books is committed to protecting your privacy. Our Privacy Policy is available online at www.eHarlequin.com or upon request from the Reader Service. From time to time we make our lists of customers available to reputable third parties who may have a product or service of interest to you. If you would prefer we not share your name and address, please check here. ☐

ROYAL AND RUTHLESS

Royally bedded, regally wedded!

A Mediterranean majesty, a Greek prince, a desert king and a fierce nobleman—with any of these men around, a royal bedding is imminent!

And when they're done in the bedroom, the next thing to arrange is a very regal wedding!

Look for all of these fabulous stories available in August 2009!

HARLEQUIN Presents

Coming Next Month

Plus, look out for the fabulous new collection
Royal and Ruthless from Harlequin® Presents® EXTRA:

HPCNMBPA0709